THE
HALLOWEEN
MASK

AND OTHER STRANGE TALES

THE
HALLOWEEN
MASK

AND OTHER STRANGE TALES

DAVID STUART DAVIES

Cover illustration: © iStockphoto.com

First published 2014

The History Press
The Mill, Brimscombe Port
Stroud, Gloucestershire, GL5 2QG
www.thehistorypress.co.uk

© David Stuart Davies, 2014

The right of David Stuart Davies to be identified as the Author
of this work has been asserted in accordance with the
Copyright, Designs and Patents Act 1988.

British Library Cataloguing in Publication Data.
A catalogue record for this book is available from the British Library.

ISBN 978 0 7509 5976 6

Typesetting and origination by The History Press
Printed in Great Britain

CONTENTS

1

THE HALLOWEEN
MASK

Ron picked himself up from the gutter. God, he felt like death. Dead drunk more like, he thought, as a knowing, twisted, inebriated grin touched his features. It was all Allison's fault. Inviting him to her Halloween party had given him hope – hope that there was reconciliation on the cards. A chance that they could get back together. The grin soured and faded. How wrong could you be, buddy? She was all eyes-on and all arms-around that advertising exec. in the shiny suit called Brian. Ron grinned again. Actually, the suit wasn't called Brian, he mumbled to himself, taking a few uncertain steps onto the sidewalk. The suit was called Melvin.

He tried to laugh at this laboured witticism, but it never came. Allison.

It was as though she had invited him to the party so that she could humiliate him. To show him that she had moved on from Ron Granger, the down-at-heel schmeel scraping a living in a jewellery store on the lower east side. Yes, she had moved on and up. Allison had graduated into the big time. To guys with shiny suits and their own expense accounts.

And so Ron had started hitting the booze. Bloody Marys – his tipple. It lessened the pain and removed certain portions of reality like an almost-completed crossword. You could see the picture but bits were missing. Reality was not complete. That's the way he liked it. The vodka told him so.

He couldn't remember leaving the party or making his way from the village towards the less salubrious part of town where he roomed.

As he left the brighter lights, he picked up speed a little and, with some determination, headed in the direction of home – or the place where his few things were and he slept nights.

'Hiya, buddy.' The voice came from the shadows. A passing pedestrian. Ron looked up and shuddered. The man's face was a skull. Black caverns rippled where his eyes should be. Fear crept upon Ron for a moment and then with sudden realisation … a Halloween mask. The guy was entering into the spirit of the evening.

Ron grinned a drunken grin. 'And boo to you, too,' he slurred.

As he passed Al's Irish Bar, the man himself, Big Alan, emerged and began lighting a large cigar.

'Hiya, Al. Enjoy the smoke,' he called, his voice strangely husky.

Al studiously stared at the cigar and ignored him.

That, thought Ron, was not like Al, but maybe he doesn't want to acknowledge a drunk in the street. I must look like a mess. He gazed down at his coat and gasped. There were several dark patches on his overcoat that looked like blood. Again, realisation took the fear away. 'Blood?' he said quietly, almost as a chuckle. 'More like Bloody Mary. Unsteady hand with the precious booze. Still, I wasn't buying.'

Finally he reached his rooming house and after some difficulty with the key – it kept slipping past the aperture – he let himself into the barren and shabby set of rooms that he called home. He slipped his shoes off and flung his coat on the chair, which was followed by his damp shirt, tie and suit.

Unsteadily, he made his way to the bathroom. As he did so his mind was suddenly awhirl with images and sounds.

The dark street.

His faltering footsteps echoing in the blackness.

The noise of a revving motorcar.

He reached the bathroom and clicked the light switch. Bright lights dazzled his eyes.

Bright lights dazzled his eyes.

The roar of the engine grew nearer.

He moved towards the sink.

He jerked his head in panic and saw that the car was almost upon him.

He gazed at himself in the mirror.

He felt the thump of the bonnet as his chest exploded.

He saw the kerb racing towards him.

Then in the mirror he saw himself. A man in a Halloween mask. A skull where black caverns rippled where his eyes should be.

But this was no Halloween mask.

2

THE
SECRET

Brian loved fishing. It was a hobby that had been nurtured by his father. The rippling water and what lay beneath its glossy surface fascinated him. By the age of ten he had become an accomplished angler and most Saturdays he and his dad would set off for Balcolme Ponds to join the other fishermen for a quiet day by the water's edge while they waited patiently for the big catch. Brian didn't mind being teased by his schoolmates that 'fishing was boring' and that he was like an old man because he enjoyed just sitting with a rod in his hand for hours on end. But Brian loved it. Even at his young age he found a strange kind of refreshing tranquillity sitting on the bank, staring at the murky water and watching the ripples sparkle in the changing light, waiting for that slight tell-tale pull on the line.

When his father died suddenly, he stopped fishing for a while, but after a couple of months, he felt the urge to be by himself again at the water's edge. He knew that it would somehow aid his grieving and he felt that his dad would want him to take up the rod again. However, he couldn't go back to Balcolme Ponds. That would be too painful. He wanted to find a stretch of water that was quiet and his alone. He wanted to be a solitary fisherman.

After a few fruitless excursions, he found the ideal spot only a few miles from home. He'd tracked through a nearby wood and then suddenly veered off the beaten track into a patch of thick undergrowth. He had no idea why he'd taken this route. Some inner force had prompted him to negotiate his way through the dense foliage. Less than five minutes later, he came to a small clearing and a stretch of placid water: a large lake. Excitement ran though him as he moved to the edge. Surely there would be fish swimming about in there, he thought, smiling for the first time in a long while. After sitting staring out onto the lake for what seemed ages, he made his way back home, determined to return the next day after school with his rod and tackle and test it out.

Within half an hour of dropping his line into the water the next day, he had made his first catch. It was only a scrappy little gudgeon, but Brian's heart burst with joy as he brought it wriggling out of the water. He had found his own lake – Brian's lake – where he could fish and be alone with his own thoughts and memories of his dad. He felt a rush of pleasure consume his body. He couldn't help it: he just laughed out loud, his voice echoing strangely across the surface of the water.

Brian went almost every day after school for at least an hour. Whether he caught anything or not didn't really matter to him. It was the act, the process of angling, that really gave him pleasure. And then one day, when he had navigated his way through the thick undergrowth – his secret route, as he thought of it – he found that there was someone else in the clearing, sitting on a rock at the edge of the lake. It was a boy about his own age. He was hunched up and looked damp. His dark hair was plastered to his head and shimmered with droplets of water. When he heard Brian approach, he turned his head to gaze at him. The boy's face was pale and gaunt, with very large eyes. He smiled when he saw Brian.

'Hello,' he said.

'Hello,' Brian replied, hesitantly.

'You come fishing?'

'Well, yes.' Brian wasn't so sure he wanted to fish now that his special place had been invaded by this stranger.

'Can I watch?'

'If you like.'

'Yes, please. I won't get in the way.'

'OK.'

Brian unpacked his tackle and readied himself to cast off.

'Are you using bait? Worms or something?'

Brian shook his head. 'Worms is for amateurs. I've got some maggots here. They're nice and plump.'

'Can I see?'

'Yeah.' He held out the jar of moist wriggling creatures.

The boy pulled a face that clearly expressed his distaste. 'They're horrible.'

Brian smiled. 'The fish love 'em.'

'Glad I'm not a fish,' said the boy. And they both laughed.

The boys sat close to each other on the edge of the lake while Brian cast off and they waited in silence to see if he would catch any fish today. At first Brian was conscious of his companion, but he soon lost himself in his own thoughts and forgot about the pale-faced boy by his side.

After half an hour, the line grew taut and began to pull slightly.

'I think you've got one,' said the boy in hushed tones.

Brian nodded and pulled gently on the line. It resisted: the sure sign that he'd hooked a fish. He tugged harder and the line fought back.

'I think it's a big one,' said the boy, with suppressed excitement.

Brian rose to his feet and pulled hard on the line, jerking up the rod and bringing his catch bursting through the surface of the lake. It was a perch. Lithe and silvery, it shone in the evening light.

'Wow,' said the boy.

'Yeah,' agreed Brian. 'I've never caught one of these here before. It's my biggest yet.'

'It must be me. I've brought you luck.'

Brian sneered good-naturedly as he reeled the fish in. 'Huh, more likely my skill as an ace angler.'

'Oh, that as well.'

Brian plopped the still-wriggling fish into his keeping net. It was a real smasher, he thought. If only his dad was here to see it.

'My name's Andrew.' The boy's voice broke into his thoughts.

Brian turned to him. 'Brian. That's my name.' And after a brief pause the two boys patted each other on the back and grinned.

They sat chatting for a while, easy now in each other's company. Strangely Brian no longer felt that Andrew was an intruder in his domain. He hadn't any real friends at school – his dad had been his best pal – and he began to enjoy the company of someone his own age. Certainly Andrew was easy to get on with.

'Will you be here tomorrow?' asked Andrew, as Brian began to pack up his tackle.

'Yes. I come most days.'

'See you then,' said Andrew staring out at the lake.

'Yeah. OK.'

And so it was that every day for over a week Brian would turn up at the lake and find Andrew waiting for him, his face beaming with delight to see his new friend. One day, as the light was failing sooner than usual and rain clouds were gathering, Brian decided to pack up early. As he was about to leave, Andrew touched his arm, gently, his features clouded with apprehension.

'What is it, what's the matter?' Brian asked.

Andrew bit his lip and turned away. 'Nothing really, I just … I just wanted to tell you …' His voice faltered.

'Just wanted to tell me what? Come on, spit it out. You can trust me. We're pals aren't we?'

Andrew smiled and nodded. 'Well it's a secret really. Do you want to know a secret?' he said in a whisper, his eyes widening.

'A secret? Yes. What?'

'Shall I tell?'

Brian gave a puzzled grin. 'Yes, tell me your secret.'

'OK. You see, I'm dead.'

'What?'

'I'm not really alive. I'm dead.' He pointed to the still flat waters of the lake. 'I drowned out there. They couldn't save me.'

Brian stared at his friend in bewilderment, but a fine tingle of fear spread up his spine.

'You're mad,' he said.

Andrew shook his head. 'It's true. I am dead. Touch my hand.' He held it out but Brian flinched. 'Go on, touch me.'

Slowly Brian reached out and laid his fingers gently on Andrew's hand.

It was as cold as ice.

'You see,' said Andrew. 'I told you.'

Brian fled. He turned and ran, thrusting himself through the thick foliage as fast as he could. The branches clutched at his clothing, scraped his face and seemingly made every effort to enfold him in their leafy embrace. When he eventually broke out into the clearing, his heart was pounding as though it would burst through his chest, but he didn't stop running, running away from the dead boy, until he reached the end of his street. Here he paused and attempted to regulate his breathing again and control his shaking body. As he made his way up the garden path, he thought his legs would give way.

His mother saw immediately that something was wrong. She ran her hand over his damp brow. 'I think you'd better get to bed with a couple of aspirin,' she said, shepherding Brian towards the stairs. He did not resist.

But he had no intention of falling asleep. He was frightened of what dreams might come when he had entered that dark realm, so he sat up in bed and let his mind relive the moments by the lake when Andrew had told him his 'secret'. There was no sense to be made of it. He remembered with terror the freezing touch of Andrew's skin, like the skin of a dead fish.

But as the shadows lengthened, he did fall asleep, into a dreamless and calm slumber. He woke in the morning refreshed and feeling strangely like that incident at the lake was something experienced by someone else. One thing was certain, he was not going there again. He was not the least bit ashamed of being frightened by the prospect.

After a day at school, Brian almost began to feel normal again. He even started to wonder whether he had imagined the whole thing at the lake. Nevertheless, he was neither brave nor foolish enough to return there. Instead, he made his way to Balcolme Ponds. He felt safe there but the once-familiar surroundings reminded him of how much he missed his dad. Vivid memories of their time together crowded his mind and he had almost forgotten about what had happened at the lake by the time he got home.

That night, he woke up suddenly. Something had propelled him from a deep sleep into cold harsh wakefulness. He sat up in bed, apprehensive and frightened, but he didn't know why. Then he heard someone mention his name – softly and sibilantly. It came from the shadows at the far side of the room. He stared at the blackness and emerging from it came a figure. A figure of a boy. It seemed to shimmer with a faint greenish glow.

It was Andrew.

'Where were you, Brian?' he said. 'I waited for you by the lake today but you didn't come.'

Brian blinked hard, hoping that this vision or whatever it was would disappear, but it didn't. It remained, shimmering and frightful in the gloom.

'Promise you will come.' The figure moved closer to the bed and as it did so the skin on its face seemed to slide off the bone. Only the eyes – those wide staring eyes – stayed in place as the flesh dribbled down its cheeks until only a damp glistening skull shone in the darkness.

Brian could not move, he could not speak and his head felt as though it would explode. Suddenly, his mind could take no more and he fell back on his pillow. He had escaped from the nightmare into unconsciousness.

The next morning he felt groggy and uncertain about what had happened during the night. He had flashes of images in his imagination – pieces of a strange jigsaw – but he was unable to piece them together to produce a complete picture.

He spent the rest of the day as though it was a dream. Voices were echoes, faces were shadows and everything seemed to be enacted in slow motion. This did not concern him. Indeed, he enjoyed the sensation. He was in his own little dreamlike cocoon.

At the end of the day, he made his way with slow deliberation to the lake.

Andrew was waiting for him by the still waters.

'I knew you would come.'

'Yes,' said Brian.

Andrew stepped forward and took Brian's hand. His touch was still ice cold but now Brian did not mind. Slowly they moved to the water's edge and stared out at the dark expanse of the lake. Brian remembered his father and those early days of fishing with him. How he had stared at the water in the same way as he did now. He was fascinated by the ripples and what lay beneath the glossy surface.

Hand in hand the two boys waded out into the lake. Further and further and further until they disappeared from sight.

3

REUNION

Eva's hand shook a little as she locked the front door. She smiled at her own nervousness. It was to be expected. It would be strange if she wasn't nervous. Well, excited really. That was the real emotion.

Door closed, she adjusted her hat and smoothed down her frock – her special frock, the one she'd bought in the January sales in anticipation of this day – whenever it would be. She hadn't realised then she'd have to wait until August before she could wear it. 20th August to be precise. Her red-letter day. Their red-letter day.

As she reached the gate she saw her neighbour Dolly Pearson returning from a shopping trip.

'Good heavens,' Dolly cried. 'You look the bees' knees. You off to the palace or something?'

Eva grinned. 'It's Tom. He's coming home today. Home on leave. I can't wait.'

'Oh, my dear, that's wonderful. How long has it been?'

Eva's smiled faded a little. 'Over a year. He's been out in the desert.'

'Well, you look a picture, I must say.'

Eva glanced down shyly. 'I wanted to look my best. Anyway, I can't stop, I'm late already.'

'Off you go, my dear, and give that gorgeous hubby of yours a hug from me.'

'I will,' replied Eva, her smile returning as she hurried off down the street.

Good heavens, thought Eva, as she pushed her way along the crowded pavement, it seemed as though the world and his wife were in London today. They really were hampering her progress. She glanced at her watch. She was five minutes late already. Oh, how she ached to see Tom again. She loved him so much. And she knew he felt exactly the same about her. What had her sister, Beatrice, said to her? 'Oh Eva, it's a marriage made in heaven.'

And so it was.

With growing excitement, Eva made her way to the edge of the pavement and stepped out into the road. The large red omnibus hit her before she knew it.

The crowds around the entrance to King's Cross Station were even denser. But she spotted Tom straight away. His tall frame and bright blonde hair made him stand out from the rest. Eva ran towards him, crying his name. When he saw her his worried features broke into a grin and he flung open his arms to receive her. They hugged tightly for a moment and then their lips met in a long passionate kiss.

'There's no one at home,' said Dolly Pearson, standing on her doorstep.

The postman looked disappointed. 'I've got a telegram for a Mrs Eva Braden. It looks official. Needs signing for.'

'She'll be back by dinnertime.'

'I can't wait around 'til then, I've got a bunch of others to deliver.'

Dolly hesitated for a moment. 'Here, give it to me, I'll sign for it.'

Dolly looked at the buff envelope lying on her kitchen table. It was official. From His Majesty's Armed Forces. What could it say? Her hand strayed towards it. She knew she shouldn't, but she couldn't help herself. Curiosity got the better of her. Gently she pulled back the flap of the envelope and extracted the telegram within. The message was simple: '... we regret to inform you of the death of Thomas Braden on August 1st, 1943 during an encounter with the enemy ...'

4

THE KEY

It came to pass that my only claim to fame now rests on my interview with the master of the ghost story: Montague Rhodes James. His last interview in fact – although he gave very few in his life. This was not out of reticence but simply that he was rarely approached.

It was 1936. I was a young and eager journalist and I wanted to make a mark as a commentator on literary affairs. I now see how foolish and naïve I was. I really didn't have the talent or perception for such a calling and after the major triumph of my interview with James, inspiration, dedication and, in truth, opportunities fell away.

It was in the spring of the year that I travelled to Eton College to meet the great man. I had become fascinated by his ghost stories as a youngster and, despite the fact that they gave me nightmares, I read and reread them with enthusiasm. They were like carefully composed paintings which on closer and renewed inspection one could perceive more terrifying detail.

I wrote an effusive missive to the Master, as I invariably referred to him, requesting an audience to discuss his art with the view to publishing the resultant interview in my paper – the now-long defunct *Essex Express*. To my surprise and delight M.R. James agreed to meet me.

I arrived at Eton College in the late morning and an ancient servant with a face and a complexion of a gargoyle directed me to the study of Montague Rhodes James. I found him dozing at his desk in the sepulchral gloom of a book-lined chamber which was illuminated solely by a brace of candelabra.

I had tapped on his door to no avail and taken the initiative to enter. As I did so the grandfather clock in the corner of the room chimed the hour. This propelled the great man to blink and raise himself from his slumber.

'Good day, young man,' he addressed me directly. There was a question in his statement, prompting me to introduce myself.

'Mr James, I am Stephen Mould from the *Essex Express*,' I said.

'Ah, yes,' he replied, his face brightening. 'My interview. Take a seat, young man and be so good as to pour us both a glass of sherry.' He indicated the decanter on his desk. I did as he asked and then the interview began.

He spoke easily and fluently in a soft dry voice, his hands fluttering before him like two desiccated butterflies when he wished to emphasise a point. I hardly had to ask him about his art – the art of the ghost story. He covered all the points I wished to raise in what was an accomplished monologue. He stressed that in creating the chills, the pleasurable uneasiness of his stories, he had to form a written pact with his reader: 'I prompt and stimulate by the framing of a horrible painting which I have lightly sketched in some of the background – but it is up to the reader to flesh out the rich and graphic detail which

I have merely suggested. That is the key to the true frightening ghost story. We each have our own personal terrors which are greater, darker, more fertile, more frightening than anything I could conceive on my own. I simply stimulate the imagination and you – the reader – take the bare bones, the hints of horror, and make them flesh. That, my boy, is the key.'

He spoke of many other things – the importance of research and atmosphere and the concerns he had at reaching out to what he described as 'the ordinary reader', but the message that stayed with me from that interview was his insistence that the effective ghost story involved a pact between the writer and the reader: the writer inspired the horrors but it was the reader who actually provided them. In this way each story became a personal interpretation.

After half an hour, he sighed heavily. 'I am rather weary now, Mr Mould. I hope you have enough material for a decent article.'

Observing that he had not touched his sherry, I said that I had. I thanked him for his time and left him sitting quietly at his desk, staring into the middle distance, lost in thought.

As I hurried down the stairs, I was met by a tall, grey-bearded fellow who gazed at me with an expression that appeared to be a mixture of surprise and alarm.

'Who are you and what are you doing here?' he asked imperiously.

'I'm Mould of the *Essex Express*. I have just been interviewing Mr James.'

His jaw dropped open in amazement. 'What nonsense,' he said mastering his emotions. 'That is impossible.'

'Why do you say that?'

'Because, sir, Montague Rhodes James died in his bed this morning at six a.m.'

I left the building, chilled and stunned at the news imparted to me by the bearded fellow. If James had died early that morning, who had I been talking to? My mouth ran dry as an answer to that question flashed in my mind. Instinctively I turned back to gaze up at the room in which I had conducted my interview. It may have been the light reflecting on the window but I thought for a fleeting moment I caught sight of the gargoyle-faced creature who had shown me up to the Master's study peering down at me. And he seemed to be smiling.

5

THE WELCOME VISITOR

The evening shadows lengthened on the blind and although she was content to sit in the dark, Dorothy switched on the small lamp by Emily's bed. She thought the artificial glow might help her sister to rally a little – but it did not. The bright light illuminated her sister's gaunt features: the grey cheeks were hollow, the skin like ancient parchment and what once had been wide lustrous blue eyes, full of vibrancy and life, were now small misty orbs. Dorothy took Emily's wrist and felt for a pulse. It was feeble and irregular. Death was but a whisper away.

That it should come to this. After all these years, thought Dorothy. All these years together, sharing. Sharing everything, including their terrible secret. But now it looked like it was going to end. It had been unthinkable once upon a time: that life, that everlasting road down which they travelled, should come to an end. But now, for Emily, it had turned into a cul-de-sac. It seemed that there was no way out and certainly no turning back. Dorothy knew that when Emily died, she would follow very quickly. Already she felt weak and emaciated. It was only her concern for her sister that kept her going. Every action was an effort. Every movement fatigued her. It seemed such a long time since they'd had sustenance. With their infirmities, the infirmities of great old age, they were no longer able to go out and obtain the necessities as they had in their glory days. They had become prisoners of their own nature.

Dorothy had often wondered whether their move to this cottage, some two miles from the nearest village, had been wise. They were now so isolated, but, of course, that had been the plan. Emily had always been keen on living as far away from people as possible, 'to prevent discovery'. But since they had come to the cottage and age had begun to catch up with them, the effort of travelling for supplies grew more onerous. Their old bones and tired bodies were not up to it. And so they were forced to fast until the situation became almost desperate and then they would make the effort once more. But this time they had waited too long and Emily had slipped into illness almost with a welcome resignation. They had both agreed that now life, their strange life, had become intolerable. Never before had they contemplated dying. Dying finally that is. It had been unthinkable, but now it seemed so real and so close. Dorothy shuddered at the thought, the thought of that eternal darkness from which there was no waking up.

She ran her fingers over Emily's icy brow. 'Oh, my dear sister,' she said, a tear rolling its way down her grey wrinkled cheek.

Then something highly unusual occurred, and for a moment Dorothy was not quite sure what was happening. The doorbell rang. Its ancient clang vibrated through the house and then it fell silent. Surely it can't be a visitor, thought Dorothy, rising uneasily to her feet. They never had visitors.

They couldn't.

More than once she had thought of contacting a doctor when Emily finally took to her bed, but she knew that would be impossible. If they were going to die, it had to be on their own terms.

And then suddenly there it was again, the metallic cacophony of the doorbell; insistent and raucous. It reminded Dorothy of the bells those creatures rang as they patrolled the streets pushing their unsavoury carts with cries of 'Bring out your dead'.

She had better answer the door in case whoever it was ringing the bell took it upon themselves to break in. 'I knew that two old ladies lived there and when they didn't answer … I thought the worst so I thought it best if I …' she could hear the explanation in her head as she went downstairs. Pulling back the rug that was rolled up on the floor to prevent the cold air seeping in, she pulled back the bolts and unlocked the door.

The feeble hall light shone upon the visitor. It was a young man, not yet twenty. He was dressed in blue jeans and wore a brightly coloured shiny blouson jacket with the words 'Pete's Pizza Parlour' emblazoned on it. He grinned a well-practised grin.

'Good evening,' he said grandly, as though he was introducing a show or a concert. 'I'm from Pete's Pizza Parlour, which has just opened in the village. We deliver pizzas and burgers within a five-mile radius and we have a special opening offer: two pizzas for the price of one.' He thrust a leaflet at Dorothy. 'Choose one off the list and I'll phone through to the shop and it'll be here in under the hour.'

Dorothy, temporarily overwhelmed by this animated performance, was about to thank the young man for the information and then ask him to leave when an idea struck her. With a gracious smile and a 'Thank you,' she took the leaflet and pretended to read it. Without her glasses the print was just a multi-coloured blur.

'Oh, these are really nice,' she said, mustering some coquettish charm. 'I think I'd like one of those and I'm sure my sister would like one, too. She's not well you know.'

'Sorry to hear that,' said the youth easily, without any conviction in his voice.

'She's in bed upstairs. I'm sure one of these pizza things would help to raise her spirits. I'll go up and see what flavour she'd like.'

'Righto.'

'Oh, I say, would you be a dear and come up with me and then when she's decided which flavour, I can pay you and it'll save me coming down stairs again.' Dorothy affected a little laugh. 'My old legs are not what they were.'

The youth seemed a little uncertain about this request but he didn't want to lose a customer – and his commission – so he nodded. 'Sure,' he said.

He trailed behind the old girl as she mounted the stairs slowly and laboriously. He had no idea that it was now her turn to put on a performance.

'In here,' Dorothy said on reaching the landing. She opened the bedroom door and the youth walked in. It was cold and musty, with a weird smell that assailed his nostrils. He saw what appeared to be a corpse in the bed: a grey, skeletal face with glassy eyes and thin lank hair peeped above the bedclothes. It was like an exhibit in the chamber of horrors and he gasped and swore. Hearing the strange new voice in the room, Emily slowly swivelled her head in the youth's direction and grinned. He swore again, his blood running cold with fear. He felt the dank atmosphere of the room rush in upon him like the beating of shrouded wings. What on earth was going on, he wondered. That was all he had time to contemplate for at that moment Dorothy hit him hard on the back of his head with a large brass candlestick, one she had bought in a German market in 1867.

The boy toppled forward on to the bed.

By now saliva was drooling down Emily's ancient chin.

'Sustenance at last,' crowed Dorothy, stepping forward and with renewed strength hauling the body further up the bed so that the youth's neck was within easy reach of Emily.

'You first, my dear. Your need is greater than mine,' she said.

Emily, now smouldering with desire, leaned forward over the youth's smooth neck. 'Thank you, sister dear,' she said. Her first words in many a long day. Then she sank her ancient fangs deep into the boy's flesh and began to drink noisily.

LUNCH WITH GRANDDAD

Mark pulled up outside the Farmer's Boy. The old pub looked exactly the same as it had when he first visited it. His mind did a quick calculation. That must have been twelve years ago. Crikey, where had the time gone? As he locked the car, he felt a ripple of pleasurable anticipation course through his body. He was almost embarrassed to be smiling. After all, he was only going to meet his granddad. As a thirty-year-old man, he should be reserving these sensations for something more important than lunch with an eighty-year-old codger. He dismissed this thought immediately. He was being unfair to both to himself and to his granddad, who certainly was not an old codger.

Granddad was a rock in his life. He had been there for him when he needed someone to talk to, someone who would listen to him without censure, making judgements or offering advice. Unburdening himself to this gentle old man was a cathartic experience and it seemed that he provided wisdom and clarity through some magical, silent osmosis. Just to observe those wise perceptive eyes and the understanding nod of the head had eased many of his challenging problems. Mark's father had died when he was in his mid-teens and this had caused his mother to withdraw into her own shell until she had become a silent witness in his life. It was when he returned from his first term at university that she had told him that his granddad wanted to meet up with him for lunch at the pub in the nearby village where he lived. Mark had gone along, not knowing what to expect and had been surprised not only at how much he had enjoyed the experience but how relaxed he had felt with the old chap. He suddenly found he could talk about things that really mattered to him: his father's death, the hole that this had created in his life and the worries and concerns he had about his academic life. His granddad nodded sagely, puffing on his pipe, his fine grey eyes focused on him.

And so began the tradition. A week before Christmas they would meet up in the Farmer's Boy and have their lunch together. It was almost like a Christmas present to Mark. He knew that whatever was on his mind, he could talk about it to his granddad.

The interior of the Farmer's Boy was cosy, quaint and idyllic. A real coal fire blazed in the hearth, a brightly decorated Christmas tree stood twinkling in the corner and a string of fairy lights decorated the bar area. Mark saw his granddad sitting in his usual place at the table in the corner, leaning back on his chair with an untouched pint of beer before him. At first glance Mark thought that he looked just the same. A little paler and thinner perhaps but not much changed. But on closer inspection, Mark could see that the old man appeared frailer than he had been last year. This was probably due to the serious illness he had suffered in the summer. But nevertheless, his eyes were as bright and keen as ever. As he turned and smiled at his grandson, Mark felt an overwhelming sense of affection for the man.

Mark bought himself a drink and joined his granddad. He was eager to tell him all about Rebecca and how he thought, at last, he'd found the one. She had seemed to come into his life from out of nowhere, but almost immediately he had realised that this was the woman that he wanted to spend the rest of his life with. After greeting the old man and wishing him a merry Christmas, Mark launched into his recital about Rebecca: how they had met, how beautiful and how intelligent she was, how supportive and how much he cared for her. In his joy and excitement, the words tumbled from him.

'I want to marry her,' he said at last. 'More than anything.'

The old man's eyes twinkled, his thin lips parted gently into a warm smile and he gave a gracious nod of the head.

Mark knew that this was his seal of approval. That was all he needed. He beamed broadly, his heart full of joy.

When the bill came, Mark pulled out his credit card before checking the details. They were handwritten on a notepad bearing the pub's name and logo: 'Christmas Lunch for One – £20.' The harsh reality of that statement brought a chill to his bones and he stared with great sadness at the empty chair across the table from him.

THE DOLL'S HOUSE

Sarah hadn't seen the doll's house in over twenty years, not since her mother had a serious falling out with Aunt Sylvia. Sarah never knew the reason for this row – she was only a youngster of ten at the time and the harsh words were whispered beyond her hearing – but the consequence was that she was no longer allowed to visit Temple Lodge, her aunt's place where she had been able to play with the doll's house, imagining that it was her own. It was a beautifully crafted replica of a Georgian mansion made some time in the late nineteenth century. It stood about three-feet high and the attention to detail was remarkable. The interior was exquisitely presented with tiny furniture and fittings and there were two mannequins inside representing the owners, whom Sarah had named Mr and Mrs Brown.

Now this rather grand model of a Georgian mansion had been delivered to Sarah's own house. It had been left to her in her aunt's will and its arrival caused Sarah a pang of guilt. She had not seen Aunt Sylvia since the rift and had not even attended her funeral. She gazed at the house which, unlike herself, had not aged at all. It still seemed the gorgeous pristine treasure of her youth. If only she had children of her own who could admire and appreciate such a magnificent plaything but Sarah, now settling into her mid-thirties, had not married and, she felt, was unlikely to. Health and certain psychological problems had made her withdraw from the mainstream of life. She was ill at ease in company and preferred her now mainly solitary existence.

She moved the doll's house into her bedroom – the softness of the room seemed to suit it. She placed it on the floor by her wardrobe and it pleased her to think that it would be one of the first things that she saw on waking.

That night, after getting ready for bed, she knelt down by her new possession and peered in all the windows. It was still as exquisite as she remembered it. Age had not taken away any of its beauty or charm. There was no fading of materials, no dust, no shabbiness, no deterioration at all. And there in the dining room, sitting at opposite ends of the dining table, were Mr and Mrs Brown, just the same as she remembered them. He was a dark-haired figure, smart in a dinner suit, with a sleek moustache and bright shiny black eyes. Mrs Brown was willowy in a chiffon gown, with blonde coiffured locks that cascaded down her back. Her features were somewhat bland apart from the bright-red lips which contrasted incongruously with her pale face.

'Nice to see you two again after all this time,' murmured Sarah and for one split second she thought she saw Mr Brown glance in her direction. She smiled at such foolishness and went to bed.

Sarah was awoken in the night by some strange noises. They were faint but penetrating. She sat up in bed and to her surprise she saw that there was a light emanating from the doll's house. Slipping on a robe, she went to investigate. As she knelt down she could see that the light was coming from the dining room. Pressing her face closer, she was shocked to see the little of figure of Mr Brown was actually moving. He had left his place at the dining table and was walking in a stiff mechanical manner towards Mrs Brown who was still sitting immobile in her chair. As he neared her, Mr Brown raised his hand and Sarah was horrified to see that he held a knife in it. As he drew closer, his robotic movements quickened and then he thrust the knife down, stabbing Mrs Brown in the chest. A small gobbit of blood oozed out of the wound and then she fell face downward on the table.

Sarah emitted a muffled scream. Mr Brown froze for a moment and then gazed up through the dining room windows at Sarah, his little face and black eyes filled with malice and hatred.

Sarah fell backwards in fright and then, like a child, scrambled to her feet and rushed back to the bed. She hid under the covers shivering with terror until sleep came to her. On waking the next morning, it took her some moments to realise why she felt so uneasy and disturbed and then she remembered. In her mind's eye she saw the little malevolent face of Mr Brown turn and stare with unguarded ferocity at her while he held the tiny knife stained with crimson.

With great temerity, she approached the doll's house once more and peered inside the dining room. Mr Brown was back in his seat at the head of the table and all seemed normal, except there was no sign of Mrs Brown. Her seat was empty and did Sarah observe minute specks of red on the delicate tablecloth by her vacant chair?

She pulled away quickly. This was all crazy, she thought. Perhaps she was going crazy. She had fought against it before and perhaps now madness was ready to claim her. What she believed she had witnessed the night before was impossible, ridiculous, a wild fantasy. It was nonsense to believe it. This was just some silly dream, an unsettling nightmare. That was all. She determined there and then to forget it altogether. Or at least push it as far back in her consciousness as was possible. During the day, whenever thoughts of the doll's house entered her head, she dismissed them immediately. It would, she thought, be mad not to do so. And she wasn't mad. She wasn't.

That night as she prepared for bed, she avoided looking at the doll's house. She had decided that the next day she would have it removed and sent away somewhere, anywhere, as long it was no longer near her. Then it would no longer be an influence. No longer a threat. At this notion, those accusative eyes of Mr Brown entered her mind and she shuddered as she fought to lose the image.

She woke suddenly in the middle of the night, feeling distressed and claustrophobic. But she didn't know why. As she sat up in bed, a sight made her cry out with alarm. The lights were on in the doll's house. And the front door was wide open. A block of pale amber light spilled onto the carpet.

The door was open.

As she sat, frozen in terror, she became conscious of a strange rustling noise like two pieces of material being rubbed together. It was rhythmic and, although faint, it was growing louder. And then she saw it. Making his way up the counterpane was Mr Brown. He strode in that strange, jerky, mechanical fashion like a clockwork toy. His head was thrust forward and those shiny ferocious eyes were focused on Sarah. They bored into her. She gave a croak of horror, but was unable to move, mesmerised by the menacing little figure. She slid down on to the pillow as he appeared over the edge of the top sheet.

'No,' she cried as he raised the tiny knife. With a swift movement he reached forward and plunged it into her right eye. She screamed loudly but not as loud as when he thrust the blade into her left eye.

She lost consciousness as Mr Brown kept on stabbing, stabbing, stabbing.

8

THE RING

The atmosphere of the Daedalus club was sombre. As an establishment for academic bachelors, the ambience was always restrained and cloister-like, the lighting sepulchral, sounds muted, and conversations hushed. And so it was on the day that Abraham Kadinsky observed a figure from his past in the gloom of the members' sitting room. He approached the man who was seated close to the fire, distractedly watching the flames.

'It's Professor Petrie, isn't it?' said Kadinsky with more than his usual enthusiasm.

The object of this effusive interrogation turned his face from the fire and gazed up at the interloper. 'It is,' he answered, in a dry, throaty voice, peering with concentration at the man who towered over him. And then, as recognition dawned, his harsh features softened a little. 'Good gracious, it's Kadinsky, isn't it?'

'Yes, sir. It must be twenty years,' he said, holding out his hand in greeting.

Petrie stared at the outstretched palm, his features darkening for a moment. With some awkwardness, he raised his arm to complete the shake. Kadinsky was shocked to see the state of his old professor's hand. He had obviously been in some kind of terrible accident. It barely resembled a human hand any more. The flesh was purple and withered, while the structure was twisted awkwardly into the shape of a damaged claw. And the index finger was missing: a small grisly stump was all that was left.

Kadinsky was unable to keep the shock from his expressive face.

Petrie gave a tired, rueful smile. 'I apologise,' he said, raising the hand. 'It is not an attractive sight is it?'

'What happened?'

Kadinsky turned his gaze to the flames again. 'What happened, indeed? Something so terrible, so difficult for the sane mind to comprehend that I am not sure myself of the answer to that question.'

Surreptitiously, Kadinsky pulled up a nearby chair and sat down by his old archaeology professor. 'Would you care to tell me?'

Petrie hesitated. Suddenly his whole body, which he had been holding in a stiff and unnatural manner, relaxed and he breathed a deep sigh. 'Why not,' he said, at length. 'It will probably do me good to relate my experience to a relative stranger – for you are a relative stranger now. We have not met for many years since we both walked the groves of academe.'

Kadinsky nodded.

'However,' said Petrie, his features falling solemn again, 'I think to begin with I would like to partake of a large brandy to help lubricate my vocal chords and provide me with enough courage to relate what you wish to hear.'

The drink was secured and Petrie took a long gulp before he began his narrative. The brandy warmed his sinews and indeed revived that spark of courage that he needed.

'Since retiring from my post at the university some three years ago, I became fascinated by the discovery of the remains of what has been commonly referred to as the Red Lady of Paviland. You may have read about of it in the press. It was a complete Upper Paleolithic-era human skeleton dyed in red ochre. It was discovered in 1823 by the Reverend William Buckland, during an archaeological dig at Goat's Hole Cave; one of the limestone caves between Port Eynon and Rhossili, on the Gower Peninsula in South Wales. The more I researched the matter, the more I came to believe that there may be other, similar bodies buried in that location. Relics of the past, long secreted by the sands of time. There was always a tendency for these ancient folk to bury their dead in groups. It seemed strange to me that no further explorations had been made at Goat's Hole Cave and so last year I took a long holiday in the region to investigate. I went seeking signs that might indicate that other burials had taken place there. I found none.

'And then one day, I ventured further into the cave than I had ever done before. To be honest it was further than it was safe to do so. I had to squat on my hands and knees to make progress. I soon began to regret my foolhardiness in persevering. I cannot tell you how oppressive, how claustrophobic the atmosphere was down there. I struggled along on my stomach with just a torch to light my way. The air was scant and foul. Then there was the cold, the damp glistening walls and the strange silence that wasn't silence at all. I lay still and listened and, God help me, I could hear …' Petrie paused, his eyes wide with apprehension.

'What could you hear?' asked Kadinsky in a thrilled whisper, leaning closer.

'I could hear ... faintly like a breeze but not a breeze ... I could hear the sound of wailing. In the flickering gloom, over the centuries, the soft cries of sorrow reached out to me. Like echoes of grief, they grew louder, invading the blackness all round me. Eventually, the sound filled my ears, drowned all my senses. I could not think. The walls, the cold damp walls, disappeared and I was blind. The wailing screams were now in my head, clamped around my brain, squeezing it to bursting point. Shadows darker than the darkness reached out to me. And then ... and then the ground gave way beneath me, and I found myself falling down a shaft. Earth and dust showered me as I rolled and twisted. I crashed down on to hard earth and lost consciousness for a while. When I came round, I was in darkness but I could hear the sea. The air was cold, damp and clammy. I had lost my torch somewhere during my fall but luckily I had a candle stub and a Lucifer in my pocket. I lit the candle and gazed around me in the strange flickering light.

'Oh, Kadinsky, imagine my wonder and joy at what I saw. It was a small chamber but the walls were adorned with crude drawings. Without doubt some were of the Palaeolithic era but others confused me. They were nothing like I had seen before. Grotesque faces and animals.'

'What a find.'

'There was more. As I moved around this chamber, not more than ten-feet square, I saw something protruding from the sandy ground near one wall. It looked like the outline of a skull. Imagine with what eagerness and excitement I placed the candle on a small outcrop of rock and scraped away the sand from the object. It was indeed a skull. An enormous skull. I scooped and dug and scraped, removing the sand away from the flinty features. But, Kadinsky, there was more than the face, more than the head. I soon discovered that there was in fact the whole skeleton.'

'Great heavens. What a remarkable find.'

'As I glanced at the guttering candle, I realised I had a limited time in which to carry out my excavations. As a result, I was more brutal and violent than I might have been in exposing … in exposing this giant. With furious haste, I pulled back the sandy soil in handfuls, to reveal the huge chest and then the legs. All was intact. A perfect specimen. He was over seven-feet tall. It was wondrous to observe, this man who had lived many lifetimes ago. And a creature who seemed to defy the history books. Of what race was he? Where had he come from and where was the rest of this giant breed?

'As I gazed down at him, something bright and shiny caught my eye. I knelt down and observed that there was a large crude ring still adhering to the bone of the index finger on his right hand. I reached out to remove it, but it seemed stuck there. I could not release it. With both hands I applied pressure to wrestle the ring from the finger. Still it would not move. In desperation, I broke the bone. It was brittle enough and I snapped it in two. The sound echoed around the small chamber. The ring was released. It was indeed a crude piece of jewellery: a brass or iron circle with a large amber stone clamped in the middle. Crude, but very beautiful.

'As I stared at the glistening amber stone, suddenly the shadows in the cave grew more erratic, glimmering in a chiaroscuro fashion. My candle was in its death throes. Common sense or perhaps some innate survival instinct told me that I had to leave while I could, while there was sufficient light for me to scramble back up the hole. I will not bore you with the details of such a tortuous and frustrating journey. Suffice it to say, after much labour and failures, I managed to claw and scrabble and eventually pull myself up to the spot where the ground had caved in. There, miraculously, I discovered my torch and was able to retrace my way back to the larger cavern. I knew that I would return. It was imperative that the skeleton was excavated properly and brought out for further study and examination. It was frustrating for me to leave but I knew I had to. At least I had the ring safely in my possession. In a moment of foolhardy vanity, I placed it on my own index finger.'

Petrie paused, took another gulp of brandy, and closed his eyes as though he were imaging the scene he had just described.

'I had not gone more than fifty yards when there was a deep rumbling within the cavern, which was followed by showers of earth. I needed no further spur to my efforts. I ran as I've never run before towards the entrance of the cave. As I did so, the ceiling of the tunnel behind me cracked and spilt. At first it rained fine dust and then, with a terrible rumbling sound, the whole roof came down. Rocks, earth and mud descended, sealing up the passageway. I just managed to stagger out into the daylight before the whole cave collapsed in on itself, sealing anything beyond the entrance in a mountain of earth and rubble. There was no doubt about it now: my giant skeleton was buried for the whole of eternity. I sank to my knees and wept.'

'How terrible,' said Kadinsky. 'Such a wonder to be found and then lost within a moment of time.' He paused and then added, 'But you still had the ring.'

'Yes,' said Petrie, coldly. 'I still had the ring.'

'There is more to your story.'

Petri nodded. 'Oh, yes, there is more. I returned to my hotel, somewhat dishevelled and deeply disappointed at the outcome of the day's events. As I prepared myself for dinner that evening, I attempted to remove the ring so that I could wash and shave, but I was unable to do so. It was lodged tight on my finger. No effort on my part could release it. I thought no more about it at that time, even when I was getting ready to retire for the evening and the ring still refused my efforts to remove it. I thought perhaps my fingers had swollen with my exertions during my adventure and by morning they would have returned to normal meaning I would easily be able to slip the ring off.

'It was a stormy night. The wind howled like a banshee and battered the French windows of my bedroom. Rain spattered against the panes like many fingernails tapping impatiently on the glass. And occasionally the room would erupt up in a violent explosion of light as a flash of lightning rent the sky. As a result, I slept badly, if at all.

'It was in the very early hours when the storm seemed to be abating that I heard it. It was faint at first and, because the wind still had some ferocity, I was not sure that I really was hearing it. But then I was sure. It was a strange, insistent click-clacking sound.

'I sat up in bed, bathed in sweat and listened intently. I knew what it was. I knew instinctively. I knew what that cursed sound was.

'It was the rattle of bones. The click, click, clack of bone against bone.

'Click, click, clack. The sound was clear now. Precise, identifiable. And near.

'Click, click, clack.

'The sound filled my brain. That click, click, clack.

'Bones moving. Compact skeletal bones scraping against each other in motion. Bones growing nearer.

'Click, click, clack.

'I stared into the gloom in desperation to see the source of the sound. As I did so, a great arc of lightening lit up the chamber and I saw before me the great skeleton from the cave. It glistened with damp and the dark eye sockets seem to glower down at me. It was within a foot of the bed and as it moved towards me in that awful mechanical fashion, there came that fearful click, click, clack of its bones.

'I fell back on my pillow in horror. I lay there, held immobile by terror as the thing leaned towards me, its white skeletal hand gasped my wrist and yanked it forward. With its other hand it pulled hard at that fatal ring with its bony fingers. The creature twisted my hand, almost wrenching it from the wrist. Pain shot through me, to every part of my body as though I was on fire, but still I could not cry out. And then, with a final tug, the creature snapped off my index finger – tore it from its root.

'My head seemed to explode with pain and I lost consciousness. When I woke up I was in the local hospital. Apparently the maid had found me the following morning lying on the bed with my mutilated hand still oozing blood.'

Petrie held up his disfigured limb. 'This is the penalty for my crime.'

'But you committed no crime,' said Kadinsky.

Petrie gave his old student a wan smile. 'We archaeologists never think of it in those terms, do we? But we are grave robbers, my boy. I was a grave robber. And in this instance the victim of the theft came back to claim what was rightfully his.'

Petrie drained the brandy glass and turned his attention once more to the flames flickering in the grate.

9

SHERLOCK HOLMES AND THE GHOST OF CHRISTMAS PAST

It was approaching the season of Christmas in the year 1899 that Sherlock Holmes was presented with one of his strangest adventures, a case which he solved in a unique fashion. How well I remember that bleak December afternoon when we received Miss Caroline Harrison in our Baker Street rooms. It had hardly grown light all day and after lunch the sky had darkened as a precursor to snow. As I lit the lamps, I gazed out of the window and watched the white flakes patter silently on our panes. It was then that we heard the bell below and shortly Mrs Hudson ushered in our visitor: a young lady of considerable beauty. She was tall with well-defined features, a porcelain complexion framed by a tumble of rich raven hair and was in possession of two of the most startling blue eyes I have ever encountered. Although it was clear to me that she was an assured and confident young woman with a strong independent streak, as she took a seat by our fireside, one could not help but observe that she was in some state of distress.

Of course this fact had not been missed by Holmes' search-ing gaze and as he addressed her, he used his softest and kindest of tones. 'I am Sherlock Holmes,' said he, taking a seat opposite the young lady, 'and this is my friend and colleague, Dr Watson.'

I nodded my head in greeting. She acknowledged this with a gentle smile.

'My name is Caroline Harrison,' she said.

'Now then,' announced Holmes in a more business-like fashion, 'any young lady who is so distracted that she dons two odd gloves before setting out in such inclement weather and has walked a fair part of the way to Baker Street …'

'How do you know that?' she asked, more with suspicion than surprise.

Holmes smiled indulgently. 'The toes of your boots are already whitened by the damp conditions and your outer coat is heavy with moisture. No doubt you had difficulty hailing a cab in the snow.'

'Quite so,' she demurred.

'Now then, Miss Harrison, if you will be so kind as to relate what is troubling you enough to bring you to my doorstep on such a harsh winter's day then perhaps I may be able to help you.'

She nodded and took a deep breath, summoning up the courage to commence her narrative. 'The matter concerns my father, Septimus Harrison, a successful stockbroker in the city. He is being haunted and I fear for his sanity.'

With a groan, Holmes flopped back in his chair. 'Miss Harrison, forgive me for being blunt, but I am a detective. I do not deal with hauntings. Ghosts and spirits from the grave are beyond my purview and, indeed, my interest. May I suggest you consult a priest or a spiritualist.'

'I say, Holmes, that's a little harsh,' I said, observing how my friend's rather brutal outburst had further distressed our visitor.

'Please, at least hear me out. The matter is not a straight-forward one: there is a mystery involved which, should it be exposed, I believe may alleviate my father's oppression.'

'Very well, Miss Harrison. I have no wish to be rude, but as I intimated, I confine my activities to this world.'

I shot Holmes a warning look. 'Let us hear your story, Miss Harrison,' I said.

'It really began a year ago. I live with my father in a town house in Kensington, my mother having died of a fever some eight years ago. I had been in the country for a week staying with friends. On my return home I found that a stranger had moved in. He was a stranger to me, that is, but my father introduced him as Oscar Leyland, an old friend of his from his youth. Apparently Leyland had been in Australia for the last thirty years where he had made his fortune. He returned to this country to settle down in his old age. It seems that he persuaded my father to let him move in with him until such a time that he could find a suitable property to purchase for his own. He was a vile man, Mr Holmes. He had thick coarse features and even coarser manners. He spoke with a harsh guttural Australian accent and was not averse to swearing even in the presence of the servants and myself. He wore gaudy checked jackets and smoked little cheroots that filled the house with an unpleasant smell. I could see that my father was unhappy to accommodate such an ill-mannered individual but I suppose he felt obliged to help out an old comrade.'

'Had you heard your father speak of this man before?'

'Never. As you may gather my father and I are very close and I know all about his life and history, but until last December I had never heard of Oscar Leyland.'

She said the name with such disdain that her lips twisted in an unpleasant fashion, robbing her face of its beauty.

'I know this is fanciful, gentlemen, but it was as though Leyland had some hold over my father. The man had only been with us a fortnight and I was beginning to find the situation intolerable. He would leer at me over the dining table and on one occasion he tried to steal a kiss when we were alone together. I slapped his face but all he did was laugh, revealing two rows of ugly broken teeth. When I complained to my father he just passed the incident off as an example of Leyland's high spirits.'

'How dreadful,' I murmured.

'Matters came to a head two nights before Christmas last year. Leyland had remained in the house all day drinking brandy. I had been out Christmas shopping and had lunch with an old school friend and, of course, my father had been at his office. Dinner that evening was a nightmare. Leyland, barely sober, slobbered over the food, hardly able to hold his knife and fork. I absented myself early and went to my room. Later I became aware of loud voices. It was the first time I had heard my father raise his voice in anger. Nevertheless, Leyland's booming tones brayed the loudest.'

'Did you hear anything of the conversation?' asked Holmes.

'A few snatches only. I remember my father saying, "You promised, you devil, you promised." And at one point Leyland roared, "But she's mine, that's all that matters."'

'Did you take the reference to "she" to mean you?'

'I honestly don't know, Mr Holmes. Events came to a tragic climax that night. I was awoken sometime in the early hours by the sound of gunshots and cries. They came from my father's private office on the ground floor. When I got there Sheridan, our butler, had also arrived. He ventured into the room, gave a gasp of alarm and emerged again quickly saying that I should not enter. I ignored his plea, brushed past him and went inside. The sight that met my eyes nearly caused me to faint. There lying on the floor were the bodies of Oscar Leyland and my father. Both had been wounded. The safe was open and the window had been smashed. It seemed that the two men had surprised an armed burglar and been shot.

'The police and the doctor were sent for. As it turned out my father had only been injured in the left arm but Oscar Leyland had been shot through the heart and was dead. The police found the gun in the shrubbery beneath the window. When my father recovered sufficiently, he recounted the incident. Apparently, he had persuaded Leyland to move out of our house to rented accommodation and was arranging to pay him one hundred pounds for his inconvenience. They had gone down to the office to retrieve the cash and seal the deal and had surprised the armed intruder, who without hesitation fired, wounding my father and killing Leyland. The burglar made a swift escape without taking anything. Despite the police investigation, he was never found.'

'Mmm,' said Holmes, staring thoughtfully at the fire in the grate, 'burglars have a remarkable facility for disappearing into thin air. But pray continue, Miss Harrison, there is more to your story, I am sure. We haven't reached the haunting yet!'

Apparently oblivious of my friend's pointed remark, Miss Harrison resumed her narrative. 'My father recovered from his injury by the early spring and he returned to work, although now he only goes to the office three days a week. I said that he had recovered from his injury. Physically he had but mentally, he became a changed man. He seems to carry around with him an unseen burden of sorrow. He jumps at the slightest noise and keeps a light burning in his room at night because he has become frightened of the dark. But just recently he has grown much worse. As the anniversary of that fateful night nears – two days before Christmas – he has begun to have delusions. He claims that he is being haunted by Oscar Leyland.'

'In what manner?'

'Apparently he appears to him in the mirror in his room. Last night I listened at my father's door and heard him talking to the ghost.'

'I assume the ghost did not reply?'

Miss Harrison shook her head. 'Of course not. I am entirely of your persuasion, Mr Holmes. I do not believe in ghosts. I am convinced that this apparition is a figment of my father's tortured imagination but it is generated by some secret he shared with that foul creature Leyland. I have tried to raise the subject with him but at the mere mention of his name my father shakes his head, refuses to talk and leaves the room. I had thought that with your special investigative powers you could find out what this "secret" might be.'

Holmes beamed. 'Now I see why you have consulted me. There is certainly a case here.'

For a brief moment the suggestion of a smile touched the young woman's tired features. 'Do you think you can help me, Mr Holmes?'

My friend steepled his fingers and brought them to his lips. 'I believe so. A plan of action is forming but I will need time and further thought before it is fully engendered. Would you call here at noon tomorrow and then we can take the matter further?'

Now the smile became a reality and Miss Harrison's eyes lit up with pleasure and relief. 'I will be here at the appointed hour.'

'Two further points. May I ask how old you are?'

'I am in my twenty-ninth year,' she replied without shyness.

'Thank you. And do you happen to possess a photograph of Oscar Leyland?'

Caroline Harrison shook her head. 'I do not have a photograph, but ...' She paused and opened her handbag and withdrew a large sheet of paper. 'Here is a sketch of the devil, which I did from memory for you. I thought it would be useful if you could actually picture the man.'

Holmes gave a chortle and took the sketch from her. 'Excellent. This I am sure will aid us into bringing this matter to a head. Now Miss Harrison, I suggest you wrap yourself up well and good friend Watson here will endeavour to secure a cab for you, eh, Watson?'

When I returned to our rooms after seeing Miss Harrison safely into a hansom, to my surprise I found Holmes engrossed once more in the book he had been reading all the morning.

'Does this mean you have already solved the mystery?' I said sitting opposite him by the fire.

'Not quite, but I believe this book may aid me in my investigation.'

'What is it?'

'It is Sigmund Freud's *Interpretation of Dreams*. As a medical man you will have heard of it.'

'Indeed.'

'It really is a fascinating analysis of how the brain can affect and indeed control our emotions, thoughts and actions.'

'You really think it can have some bearing on this case?'

'Yes, I do, Watson. I do.'

The next day dawned cold and bright. The snow had ceased to fall, but it left behind a crisp white covering that decorated the city in readiness for Christmas. Holmes had gone out on some errand or other shortly after breakfast and I spent the morning alone. He returned just before noon at which time Miss Harrison arrived with an eagerness to learn what conclusions my friend had reached concerning her dilemma. In typical fashion Holmes had not discussed the matter with me and so I had no idea what he was about to say to his client.

'With your permission I should like to conduct an experiment this evening, Miss Harrison, on the anniversary of the death of Oscar Leyland', he said once the young lady was seated by our cheery fire. 'And to carry out this experiment, I shall require your assistance.'

'I'll do anything, if it will resolve matters,' she said firmly.

Holmes gave a quick smile. 'I thought you would say that. I need to gain access to your father's bedroom this evening without him being aware. Could that be arranged?'

Miss Harrison thought the matter over. 'We usually dine at seven-thirty, after which it has become my father's habit to retire to his bedroom. I believe he reads a little before going to bed. I could make sure the back door is left open during our meal which would present you with the opportunity of entering the house and slipping upstairs to his room.'

Holmes rubbed his hands together. 'Excellent! You can provide me with a sketch map of the house. I must be sure that I enter the correct room.'

'Of course.'

Suddenly Holmes' face became very serious. He reached out and took the young woman's hands in his. 'I have a strong belief that this evening I can uncover the truth, the secret, as you call it, which has brought distress to your father. However, I shall be using the most unconventional method in order to do so. I have to warn you that should I be successful, I cannot guarantee that the outcome will be joyous.'

She nodded gravely. 'I understand. I feel that anything, any truth will be easier to bear than this dreadful uncertainty that is driving my father to an early grave.'

'This is one occasion when I shall not require your services, my dear Watson. I must carry out this little investigation on my own,' Holmes informed me after our visitor had left. Seeing my disappointed expression, he smiled and patted me on the shoulder. 'Fear not, I will present you with all the details on my return. And there is one thing you could do which would be of the greatest assistance …'

'Anything.'

'I estimate that it will be between midnight and one in the morning when I return. I will not have had dinner and so a little late supper would be most welcome. As it will be in the early hours of Christmas Eve something festive would be most appropriate with a good bottle of claret to wash it down. Would you be so kind as to arrange that?'

'Yes,' I said with some disappointment, not happy at being left on the sidelines in one of Holmes' investigations.

He spent most of the afternoon in his room, emerging around five o'clock. He had retired as the tall, upright, clean-shaven fellow lodger with the keen aquiline features and swept-back hair that I knew so well, but he reappeared as a bloated grotesque fellow with a balding pate and fiery side-whiskers. He shambled towards me, dressed in cord britches and a vivid checked jacket.

I gasped at this transformation. I had seen Holmes in many disguises but this, I believe, was his greatest triumph. He was the very image of Oscar Leyland as sketched by Miss Harrison.

Holmes smiled at my astonishment, revealing a row of ugly and broken teeth. 'Well, I must leave you, my friend; I have some haunting to see to.'

Without another word he swept from the room. I moved to the window and saw him emerge into the snow-bedecked Baker Street moving swiftly down the pavement in search of a cab.

I spent the night between bouts of reading one of Clark Russell's seafaring tales and skimming through the pages of Freud's *Interpretation of Dreams* in an attempt to determine what my friend had planned this evening. As the clock chimed midnight I was no wiser. As the minute crept past the quarter hour, I gazed at the festive cold supper on our dining table that Mrs Hudson had prepared for us along with the inviting bottle of claret and I was tempted to start the meal without Holmes. As my hand reached for the corkscrew, I heard a foot on the stair. The door burst open and a dishevelled fellow, half in and half out of his disguise, crossed the threshold.

'Holmes,' I cried, relieved to see him.

He grinned at me and I was pleased to see that he had discarded the grotesque dentures he had worn earlier that evening.

'It is over,' he said.

Some five minutes later, with all vestiges of his disguise removed, Sherlock Holmes was his old sleek self again. Wrapped in his mouse-coloured dressing gown, he sat opposite me by the fire, sipping a glass of claret.

'I beg you, keep me in suspense no longer,' I said eagerly.

Holmes nodded. 'It has been a most instructive affair, my friend. As you are well aware from the outset I knew that whatever kind of dark shadow haunted Septimus Harrison it did not have its origin in the realms of the supernatural; rather it was some real and tangible ghost from the past. And quite obviously that ghost was Oscar Leyland. He disappeared from Harrison's life over thirty years ago and then he suddenly returns posing a threat to the stability and serenity of his household. Why? What was the hold Leyland had over Harrison? One could only surmise and certainly I came up with several theories to explain the situation. But those snatches of conversation which his daughter relayed to us helped me narrow down the matter. You remember, she heard her father exclaim, 'You promised, you devil, you promised'; and Leyland responded with, 'But she's mine, that's all that matters.' I deduced that the promise was for Leyland to leave Harrison and his family alone. Why? Well because in some way 'she', that is Miss Caroline Harrison, was his. In what way, you might ask. In the only way possible given the thirty-year absence and the fact that Miss Harrison is twenty-nine.'

'Great heavens ... you mean that she was his daughter!'

'That's how I read the riddle. This morning I visited the various shipping lines to check the passenger lists from Australia to this country in the November and December of last year. I discovered that the SS *Gerontes* docked at Southampton on 25th November 1898 with a certain Oscar Leyland on board. However, the gentleman in question was travelling third class – hardly the means of travel for a rich man. Obviously he had returned to this country penniless and was intent on securing a home and finances from Septimus Harrison because he had some hold over the poor devil.'

'Caroline was really Leyland's daughter.'

'Yes. It has the hallmarks of a Greek tragedy doesn't it? It also became clear to me that the scenario of the attempted robbery was a set up in order for Harrison to kill Leyland. And so it turned out to be.'

'How do you know for certain?'

'Because Harrison told me tonight. In reading Freud, I became convinced that the apparition of Leyland that Harrison claims to have seen was merely a projection of his own guilt and so I reasoned that if I could impersonate this ghost I could elicit a confession from the man, thus relieving him of his terrible burden. That is what I did. When Harrison retired to bed, I was waiting for him in his room, secreted behind a curtain. He nearly fainted when I emerged from my hiding place but he was soon pleading for forgiveness. With gentle prompting on my part, he revealed the full story of his tragedy.

'Over thirty years ago Harrison and Leyland sought the affection of a young woman called Emily. She was torn between them but one night Leyland forced his attentions upon her. He then deserted her once he knew she was bearing his child. Septimus Harrison offered to marry the girl and take the baby as his. He also paid for Leyland's passage to Australia and gave him the sum of five hundred pounds to help establish himself there on the promise that he would never return England. Then last year, like some phantom, he returned to blackmail Harrison into providing him with shelter and money. He threatened to tell Caroline that she was in fact his daughter if Harrison did not comply.

'The situation became intolerable for Harrison and so he lured Leyland to his office in the house in the small hours with the promise of more money. He had already faked a burglary scene when Leyland entered. Harrison then shot his tormentor dead before wounding himself to add to the authenticity of the burglary story.'

'It is fantastic.'

'We often forget how often the thread of the fantastic runs through what are perceived as ordinary lives,' said Holmes, draining his glass. 'Harrison confessed all to my disguised persona. Then it was time to reveal myself. By now the fellow was drained of emotion and my revelation prompted little reaction. I could see that by his open confession the weight of guilt had been lifted from his shoulders.'

'But the man is a murderer.'

'In the eyes of the law, yes. Man-made law. But what he did was to protect the happiness and sanity of his innocent daughter, to protect her from the clutches of a heartless and evil man. I for one cannot condemn him for that. I believe that he has suffered enough. I promised him that I would keep his secret. I told him that neither his daughter nor the authorities would ever learn the truth from me.'

I raised my eyebrows in surprise.

'Apart from this one act, Septimus Harrison has lived a good and blameless life and certainly he will not transgress again. And after all, my dear Watson, it is the season of forgiveness. Now, pour me another glass of this superb claret and then let us attack the excellent cold supper that you have arranged for us.'

As we repaired to the dining table, I asked Holmes what he had told Miss Harrison of the case.

'Nothing. As I left the house I informed her that the matter was settled but that detectives like magicians have their procedures which must remain secret. I assured her that her father will be haunted no more. That brought a smile to those careworn features. Now my dear fellow as we have passed into the hours of Christmas Eve, may I raise my glass and wish you a very merry Christmas.'

10

I KNOW
WHAT YOU DID

Raymond had just drained the whisky glass when the telephone rang.

'Hello?'

Since he'd been living on his own after Helen's death he had got out of the habit of giving his full name and number. What do they want, he thought, the story of my life?

It was one of his newfound freedoms.

He waited for a response. There was a long hissing silence.

'Hello,' he said again, this time the irritation was quite clear in his voice.

'I know what you did,' came the response, breathy and faint.

'What?'

Click. The dead phone burred.

Raymond still held the receiver close to his ear, frozen with puzzlement, a frown deepening his brow.

The second call came in the middle of the night. Raymond had just won the struggle to get off to sleep, aided by pills and whisky, and the shrill cry of the bedside phone dragged him back to groggy consciousness. His arm flailed about for the lamp switch, knocking the empty tumbler from the table by his bed. It thumped softly on to the carpet. Eventually grabbing the phone, he fell back on his pillow. 'Yeah?' he said, half awake, his mouth dry and voice muffled.

'I know what you did.'

It was the same caller, the same breathy, sinister intonation.

The same message.

Raymond broke out into a cold sweat as he tried to pull himself together, but the alcohol and the Nembutal fought back, fogging his brain.

'Who are you?' he said at length.

There was an unpleasant chuckle and then, 'I know what you did and you won't get away with it.'

'What d'you mean?'

But it was too late: the phone went dead again.

'Oh, my God,' he groaned, letting the receiver slip from his limp grasp.

Raymond felt better in the morning. The pale blue sky and the early sunshine helped him put the calls in perspective. It was a crank. Obviously. Some lonely loony who got his kicks from ringing strangers and trying to frighten them. Yes, of course, that was it. No doubt he would be one of the many this saddo had telephoned last night. Raymond even managed to smile as he poured himself a second cup of tea and indulged in a third slice of toast, smothered in butter. Another little treat. Not like in the old days, eh? His smile broadened. That was it, he thought, as he crunched his toast, his mind returning to the calls: they were the work of some weird fellow with nothing better to do. Case closed.

Indeed, that is exactly how it appeared. There were no further disturbing calls that week until Raymond had almost forgotten about them. He no longer flinched when the phone rang and he no longer let his hand hover hesitantly over the receiver wondering whether to answer it or not, while his stomach tightened into an aching knot.

It was eight days after the second call that he received the third. He was watching a porn movie on DVD when the phone rang. With a grunt of annoyance, Raymond freeze-framed the action on screen and went to answer it.

'Hello,' he barked into the mouthpiece.

As soon as he heard the hissing silence he knew it was the crank caller.

'I know what you did.'

'Get lost, will you!' Raymond bellowed and was just about to slam the receiver down when the caller spoke again.

'Your wife ... you killed her. Didn't you?'

Without thinking what he was doing, Raymond let the receiver fall back in the cradle. For a moment his mind went blank and then he groaned. 'He knows. My God, he knows,' he mumbled and slumped against the wall, he brow wet with perspiration.

Indeed, when his heartbeat had reduced itself to the rhythm of a road drill, this was the conviction that lingered in his thoughts. The caller, whoever he may be, knew that he had murdered his wife.

It had been easy. Surprisingly so. Helen, overpowering, demanding, proscriptive Helen – the young girl with the bright eyes and pert bosom who had transformed into his matronly probation officer. There had turned out to be more rules and regulations in her regime at No. 41 Orchard Avenue than there had been in the Third Reich. Even now he shuddered to think of her. It had been … what was the word … essential … necessary … imperative to his surviving that she didn't. So, it had been easy: she had a weak heart and he had an enquiring mind. Obtaining the foxglove leaves had been tiresome but worthwhile. The old digitalis administered in hefty but disguised doses had done the trick very nicely. The ball and chain had been severed. Now she was dead and he was free – until now.

He headed for the kitchen and the whisky bottle. A hard slug warmed him, the fire radiating from his empty stomach helping to clear his muddled mind. 'All right, Raymond,' he told himself, 'you've been found out. Some creep knows you did your wife in. But who? Who could possibly know you wanted her out of the way? The public face of the marriage was smooth without any visible cracks. You'd never expressed any disloyal feelings to anyone but yourself. What about Helen? If she had an inkling of the hatred she'd engendered in you – which was difficult to believe, so insensitive was she of others' feelings – who would she have confided in? The answer instantly snapped back at him: her brother. Of course, her miserable, unstable brother, Robert. Once Raymond had reached this conclusion, he was quickly reminded of the searching, piercing glances that Robert had given him at Helen's funeral. They had hardly spoken a dozen words, but oh that fierce, reproachful stare.

Another swig of whisky.

Strangely, Raymond felt somewhat relaxed now that he knew who the phantom caller was. Obviously Robert was not after cash, but a confession. Well, like sister, the brother would have to go, too. This raised the question, how? What method could be used to rid him of this threat in his life?

Suddenly his thoughts were disturbed by strange, loud sounds from the sitting room. It was the DVD cutting off freeze-frame and slipping into the noisy movie. He grinned.

'Hello?'

'I know what you did. You killed your wife.'

'Please, please leave me alone,' moaned Raymond, his voice throbbing with fear, while his eyes sparkled with mirth. He replaced the receiver beaming. He even afforded himself a brief chuckle. 'Enjoy your few moments of pleasure, Robert. Enjoy them … before you join Helen.'

Raymond, with that enquiring mind of his, had a new subject to research: motor mechanics. He spent two days in the local library with notebooks and a flask of tea, delving into the mysteries of the internal combustion engine and in particular brake-fluid pipes. He was a quick learner and now, with his mind brimming with knowledge and his notebooks full of detail, he was ready to move on. He no longer required the whisky crutch and he slept well at night. He received just one more call from Robert before he was ready to act – to put his new-found knowledge to practical use.

On the following Friday night, appropriately equipped, Raymond visited Robert's house. He knew that the back door to his garage had a faulty Yale lock and he would have no trouble gaining entry. So it proved. The job of draining the brake fluid was remarkably simple and he was back home in his own bed well before dawn broke.

'Robert? Raymond here. Sorry to call you so early, especially on a Saturday morning; I know how precious your weekends are. It's just that I've got to see you urgently. Something about Helen. It's been preying on my mind since her death. I think I'll go mad if I don't talk to someone.'

Despite Robert's murmuring words of concern, Raymond could not help but detect the note of excited pleasure in his voice.

'Could you see me this lunchtime? No not here. Not … in Helen's home. I thought if we could meet in the Quarry Arms off Stansfield Road. You know the one; it's set back to the right at the bottom of that steep hill. Please say you'll come. Oh, thank you. I'll see you there about one o'clock. Bye.'

As Raymond sipped his whisky in the lounge of the Quarry Arms, he realised that it was his first drink in nearly a week, since he'd thought up his master plan, in fact. He raised his glass in a silent toast to Robert, soon to join his dear sister. He had great difficulty in stifling a giggle. One or two customers at the bar turned to look at him and he quickly grabbed a local newspaper from a nearby seat to hide behind. He glanced at his watch: 12.45. Not long now.

Idly he scanned the items in the paper. They were the usual potpourri of unsensational stories typical of all local rags: reports on an amateur drama production; schoolchildren raising money in a charity appeal; old lady mugged on the way home from church. But there was one item that caught Raymond's eye. Indeed the story leapt off the page at him, causing him to spill some of his drink.

'Telephone Nuisance Caught' ran the headline. Raymond's eyes ran speedily over the story. Apparently lonely teenager Darren Firth had been ringing a series of widowers in the locality, whose names he had obtained from the *In Memoriam* column, saying that he knew they had killed their wives. He had fallen into a trap set up by the local constabulary and British Telecom. He was now in police custody, awaiting a psychiatric report.

Raymond's mouth gaped open and his throat felt very dry. He dropped the paper and for a few moments the bar lounge swam before his eyes.

Suddenly the door of the public house crashed open and a large fellow in a dark overcoat burst in. 'Quick,' he bellowed at the barman, 'Call the police and ambulance. There's been a terrible accident. Car went out of control coming down the hill. Looks like his brakes had failed. It smashed bang into the wall at the bottom. It's a real mess. Looks like the driver is a gonner'.

Later that evening, Raymond sat at home cradling a large glass of whisky in his hands, while staring blankly into space. He felt numb and empty. What had he done? And all for nothing.

The telephone rang shrilly, cutting the silence like a knife.

For a moment he hesitated and then shakily raised the receiver to his ear. 'Hello?'

There was a hissing silence and then a breathy voice said: 'I know what you did.'

11

THE FLY
HOUSE

W hy The Fly House?'

Tom jumped out of the car and gazed at the whitewashed cottage embraced by sweeping lawns and fulsome foliage. It looked as though it had been abandoned to the encroaching greenery and as such was just what Tom had hoped for. It was to be their French pied-à-terre for ten days: the restful summer vacation both he and his wife Ruby needed desperately. It had been a tough old year and they were both a little ragged around the edges.

Ruby joined him, gazing at their new temporary home, smiling with satisfaction at the prospect.

'I've no idea why it's called The Fly House, but it's very pretty,' she said, linking her arm through Tom's.

'I fully expected some sort of conservatory stuck on the end with a whole lot of angled windows looking like the eyes of a giant fly.'

Ruby laughed. 'Let's unload the car and get unpacked, then a glass of something alcoholic, eh?'

Tom nodded with a grin.

'Now, I know why it's called The Fly House. The buggers are everywhere. I've just killed half a dozen of them in the sitting room.'

'Good for you, darling,' Ruby observed dryly as she struggled to open the bottle of champagne they had brought all the way from England. It had been in the fridge less than an hour, while they had unpacked and explored their holiday pad, but now it was time for their celebratory drink.

After an echoing pop and an enthusiasm of foam, she poured a generous measure of champagne. 'You won't notice the little buzzing things once you've got your mouth round a glass or two of champers.'

'Too true,' Tom grinned, before taking a quick slurp. 'And what pray are you going to rustle up for tonight's feast?'

Ruby raised her eyebrows in disdain.

'Is there a can of Raid or some such French fly killer in the kitchen cupboard? These bastards seem to be multiplying. I've killed another eight of the things in the sitting room since I last saw you. I've splattered several against the windowpane with our guide to France.'

'Murderer,' cried Ruby, draining the pasta.

Tom investigated the cupboard under the sink.

'Aha!' he cried in triumph. 'Here we are. My French is dodgy but reading the instructions I reckon this brings a painful death to anything that creeps, buzzes or flies.'

Snatching up the red and yellow aerosol can, Tom headed for the sitting room, where after a short time Ruby could hear the violent gush of the deadly spray followed by gleeful cries of 'Gotcha!' at regular intervals.

'There's another one,' cried Tom, dropping his knife and fork and reaching over for the aerosol can on the sideboard.

'Oh, for Heaven's sake,' said Ruby, taking a swig of red wine, 'it's only a harmless fly.'

'There's no such thing,' Tom replied as he watched the creature plummet to the floor where it wriggled in its death throes. Calmly he crushed it under his heel.

When they went upstairs that night, Tom took the aerosol spray with him and placed it on the little cane table by the side of his bed.

'How romantic,' muttered Ruby, pulling the sheets up around her neck. 'Are you going to keep an all-night vigil on fly-squirting duty?'

'Just being prepared, my love. You know how much I hate flies.'

Tom woke in the dead of night and felt very strange.

His skin tingled and his throat felt incredibly dry. In fact, as he opened his mouth to speak, he seemed to gag on something. He was overcome with a choking sensation. With great difficulty, he pulled himself up in bed in the darkness – a darkness that was unnatural; and unnervingly complete.

He rubbed his eyes and his fingers encountered a strange crustiness. Instinctively he clamped his hand to his face and felt a brittle undulating presence there. It was then that he became aware that in the silence of the night, there was a fierce penetrating buzzing sound which seemed almost to be coming from inside his head. He tried to cry out in shock and surprise but to his horror he discovered that his mouth was filled with some thick wodge of moving matter.

Flies.

My God. There were flies. Hundreds of them.

Blindly he pulled the covers from himself and tried to stand. As he did so he banged against the table at his bedside and the lamp crashed to the floor, but he could neither see nor hear it.

The noise woke Ruby and she clicked on her bedside light. She screamed when she saw her husband staggering across the bedroom, like a zombie. His head was an undulating black mass that rippled like a seething iridescent hood. Gruff inarticulate noises emanated from him as he blundered forward, his hands wildly brushing his face.

With horror she realised that his head was encased in a moving mask of black buzzing flies. And as he rubbed his face in a frantic attempt to dislodge them, more of the creatures took their place, sealing his face in darkness.

A bleak crawling darkness.

He was conscious now of the filthy creatures making their way down his windpipe and into his lungs; into the canals of his ears and clogging his nostrils.

Like a man on fire, he crashed through the bedroom door and floundered onto the landing where he missed his footing and fell headlong down the wooden stairs. There was a snap when his neck broke.

As he lay there, his lifeless body twisted awkwardly at the bottom of the stairs, the flies buzzed around him in victory.

12

THE LADY IN THE GARDEN

M ummy, who is the lady in the garden?'

Sally Drury looked up from her morning paper. 'What did you say, darling?' She smiled across at Becky, who was staring out of the window.

'There's a lady in our garden and she seems to be waving at me.'

'Is this one of your little tricks, young lady?'

'No, no. She's really there.'

Sally rose from the breakfast table and joined her daughter by the window.

'Where is she?' asked Sally, as she scanned the empty lawn before her.

'I think she just moved behind the willow tree.'

'And I think you're playing one of your funny games again, Miss Rebecca Drury.'

'No, honest, mummy. The lady was there.'

'Well, she's not there now,' observed Sally tartly, checking her watch. 'And it's time you got yourself ready for school or we'll both be late. Come on scamp. Chop, chop.'

Later that night, Becky was hiding under her bedclothes with a torch reading one more chapter of Harry Potter. Her mother let her read until nine o'clock but then insisted Becky went to sleep and turned all the lights out. How can you go to sleep, Becky told herself, when you just needed to find out what happened to Harry and his friends? She had smuggled a torch into her room and after she'd heard her mum go downstairs, she continued the Potter saga under the sheets.

After about an hour, her eyes were beginning to droop and she realised that she'd have to give up reading now. She placed the book on the floor and then slipped out of bed to stash the torch in the bottom of her wardrobe ready for the next night. As she did so, she felt herself strangely drawn to the window. Pulling back the curtain, she gazed down into the garden below. There was a full moon and it illuminated the garden as though a creamy spotlight were trained on it. She stared for some moments at the old willow tree, wondering if the lady she had seen that morning was still there, hiding in the shadows.

And then she was suddenly there, standing on the lawn in the full moonlight. She was a grey figure and her features were indistinct, masked by the sharp shadows cast by the moon. The lady seemed to be gazing up at Becky's room, her arms held out as though in supplication.

Although Becky couldn't see the face clearly, she knew there was something wrong with it. Something terribly wrong. She pressed her own face against the cold windowpane to see more clearly. Three dark apertures stared back at her: the lady seemed to have three eyes. Becky shuddered. The creature glided across the lawn until she was directly under

Becky's window. The young girl pulled away in fear, but again was drawn back as though hypnotised by those three eyes.

But they weren't three eyes. The third dark shape in the centre of the lady's forehead was not an eye. Of course it wasn't. It was a wound. A savage round wound, and as she gazed at it in horror, she saw a liquid seep out of the wound and trickle slowly down the woman's face like the trail of some hideous insect. The blood, for that is what Becky thought it was, continued to flow until the woman's face was completely covered in it. The creature opened her mouth in a silent scream.

Becky ran back to her bed and hid whimpering under the covers for what seemed like forever until, mercifully, sleep overtook her.

At breakfast the following morning Sally Drury noticed that her daughter was not her usual chirpy self. Indeed, she looked tired and drawn.

'You OK, baby?' she asked, rubbing her hand on the back of her daughter's head.

Becky nodded, casting a furtive glance towards the kitchen window. Dare she look out? Dare she see if the lady was still there? But her nerve failed her and she ran to the hall to collect her coat and school bag. The sooner she left the house the better.

'Remember Grandma's coming round to make your tea tonight,' Sally said as she bundled her daughter into the car. 'I'm going to be doing some late-night shopping.' She grinned and added, 'Late-night Christmas shopping.'

Sally had expected her daughter to react at the mention of Christmas and the possibility of presents, but instead she stared down at her school bag. I hope she's not coming down with something, thought Sally as she slipped the car into gear to reverse it down the drive.

Town was really busy that evening, the pavements crowded with shoppers caught up with the Christmas fever. There were carol singers and various stalls selling hot drinks and snacks and even one or two itinerant Father Christmases collecting for charity. Sally quite enjoyed the atmosphere and allowed herself to be caught up in the festive mood. Her shopping excursion had been successful: she had managed to buy most of what she had intended. Her last port of call was the little jewellers in the small side street off the market square where she intended to treat herself. She had seen a pair of pearl earrings in the window weeks ago and coveted them – whenever she was in town she had found an excuse to pass by the jeweller's window to look at the earrings.

Well, she deserved it. It had been a hell of a year, what with the divorce and everything.

The shop was empty and dimly lighted. An elderly lady came from a back room to serve her.

'They are lovely, aren't they?' she said, bringing the earrings to the counter for Sally to inspect.

As she was doing so the door opened and in walked Father Christmas. The two women turned and gazed at him with amusement, but their smiles disappeared quickly when they saw that he had a gun in his hand.

'Empty the till and be quick,' he snapped, waving the weapon at the two women.

'Don't be stupid,' said Sally taking a step towards the intruder. 'You can't do this.'

'Don't come any closer,' he said, his voice cracking slightly. It was clear to Sally that this Father Christmas was hardly out of his teens.

'I said don't be stupid. Give me the gun before you do something you regret.' She held out her hand and moved closer.

'Get back!' the youth cried, his eyes wide with alarm. 'Get back!' And then he fired.

Sally heard a large explosion. She opened her mouth to scream, but no sound came out and then the swift darkness of death claimed her. She fell to the floor, the gaping wound on her forehead glistening with blood.

Becky had gone to bed early. She had felt unwell all day and couldn't get the image of the lady in the garden from her mind. She tried reading Harry Potter but she couldn't concentrate and so she turned the lights out and attempted to go to sleep. Lying in the darkness, she thought she could hear someone crying. It was an unnerving stifled intermittent moan. Despite her better instincts, she rose from the bed and looked out into the garden. To her relief, the garden, frosting over now in the chill, was empty.

And then she was conscious of a movement behind her. In the shadows. She turned and saw the figure. It was the lady from the garden. She was now in the house. Becky froze as the apparition moved towards her, her arms outstretched. As her face emerged from the shadows, Becky saw again the terrible bleeding third eye in the centre of her forehead, but what made the young girl's heart constrict with terror and fear was that now she could see this lady's features quite clearly for the first time.

Her mind numb with horror, Becky uttered a single word: 'Mummy.'

13

THE STIGMATA SKULL

Emilia Featherstone paused on the staircase and gazed out of the window down on the grounds of Brookfield Hall and sniffed. As she suspected, Jonas was not keeping them up to standard. The autumn leaves littered the pathways in untidy multi-coloured heaps and the lawned areas obviously hadn't been cut in some time. By now the December dampness had sodden the turf and it would not be possible to do anything with it until the spring when, no doubt, it would be past salvaging.

She sniffed again and this time there was no mistaking the disapproval in the gesture. Her gaze dropped to the windowsill and observed the dust there. Her nose wrinkled as she drew a gloved finger across it, trailing a jagged line through the dirt.

She heard movement behind her and, turning, she saw her nephew, Jonas Blackstock, struggling up the stairs with her luggage.

'Really, you should have got Braithwaite to do that. It's his job after all and quite honestly you haven't the brawn for it.'

Jonas forced a smile and released the two large cases on to the landing. 'Braithwaite's not here at the moment, I'm afraid. He was called away suddenly. His brother is very ill.'

'How terribly inconvenient. These people have no sense of timing.'

'Well, let's get your bags up to your room, eh?' Once more Jonas grappled the two cases and, with a certain amount of huffing and puffing, mounted the final set of stairs ahead of his aunt Emilia.

'Your usual room,' he said, throwing the door open to reveal the large but gloomy candlelit bedroom. A meagre fire sputtered in the grate. This was the chamber she used when she made her bi-annual visits, in the spring and autumn, to Brookfield Hall. It was a promise she had made, unwisely she now thought, to Jonas' parents before they died. She had never cared much for the young man but since he had inherited the hall and the Blackstock fortune he had behaved in a scurrilous and spend-thrift fashion, indulging in his passion for fleshly pleasures and his interest in the black arts, demonology and witchcraft. He had claimed that he was making some kind of intellectual study of the subject, but Aunt Emilia had other suspicions.

She stepped inside the bedchamber, surreptitiously running her finger along the sideboard. To her dismay, it made a furrow in the dust.

'Is your housemaid away visiting a sick relative as well?' Aunt Emilia asked with sarcastic sternness.

Jonas chuckled nervously. 'Actually Matilda gave her notice a month ago and I haven't managed to get round to replacing her yet. You know how it is.'

'I am afraid I do not. An efficient and well-run house needs reliable servants. There is a distinct air of neglect about Brookfield since my last visit. Tell me, how many of the staff are still here?'

'Well …'

'Come now, Jonas: the truth. Will Mrs Craven be cooking our dinner this evening?'

The young man shook his head. 'I am afraid not. But I have prepared a very nice chicken dish.'

'You! And what of Mrs Craven?'

'She became difficult. Wanting more money. I had to let her go.'

Aunt Emilia sat on the edge of the bed and sighed. 'If your poor mother could see the place now … Oh, Jonas.'

'Don't worry Aunt, I have plans to sort out everything out.'

'What plans?'

Jonas chuckled again. 'Plans. Things will be a little basic for you on this visit, but in the spring when you return, you'll see a great improvement.'

Aunt Emilia gave her nephew a stern glance. She didn't believe a word he had said.

'I'll leave you now to unpack and I'll light a big fire in the sitting room.' He left swiftly before she could criticise him further. However, he had only reached the top of the staircase when he heard a cry of alarm and his name being called out. He rushed back to the bedroom to find his aunt staring at an object placed at the centre of a small table situated by the window.

As he entered her arm shot out, her bony forefinger pointing at the object.

'What on earth is that dreadful thing?'

'Oh, my skull, you mean. It is a little curio I bought on one of my trips to London. It rather took my fancy.'

'It is revolting.'

Jonas smiled and picked up the skull, causing his aunt to flinch and take a step backwards.

'It is a stigmata skull. Well, that's what the funny little fellow who sold it to me called it. It's supposed to have magical properties. All a lot of nonsense, of course.'

'A stigmata skull? I don't understand.'

Jonas caressed the top of the skull. 'It is able to foretell death.'

'What a horrible idea. How?'

'Its eyes bleed. They bleed real blood. If you gaze at the skull and see the eyes bleed you are doomed to die.'

Aunt Emilia's hand flew to her mouth to stifle a gasp. 'So you thought you'd leave it in my room.'

Jonas shook his head, greatly perturbed. 'No, no not at all. I put it there after I bought it in the summer. To be honest, I forgot it was in here. I didn't mean to upset you.'

'Well you have. Get it out of my sight immediately Take the foul thing away from me.'

'Of course, Aunt.' Clutching the skull to his chest, Jonas scurried away.

The dinner that evening was a disaster. Aunt Emilia, wearing a very heavy shawl over a thick velvet gown, constantly complained of being cold and left most of the meal, declaring it inedible. Jonas plied her with wine regularly, hoping that would ease her temper, but it had little effect on her demeanour. It just caused her to slur her words slightly.

As the candles and the fire burned low, Aunt Emilia seemed ready to retire for the night, but just as Jonas thought she was about to return to her room, she uttered a very audible sigh and leaned forward on the table, her arm outstretched, the imperious finger pointing at Jonas.

'You have got yourself into a mess, haven't you, boy?'

'A mess?' The surprise in his voice was unconvincing.

'When your parents died and left you this house and a respectable fortune, I thought you would abandon your recklessly extravagant behaviour and take on some employment. It needs brains, industry and care to maintain a house like Brookfield. I expected you to behave in a sensible manner, not keep wandering up to London buying phenomenally expensive rare books and weird artefacts – such as stigmata skulls. But the evidence suggests otherwise. No matter how feebly you have tried to cover it up, you now have no money left to employ your household staff – butler, gardener, housemaid, cook. They are all gone. Isn't that so? You are now in those proverbial dire straits … without a canoe or whatever that wretched phrase is.'

Jonas nodded meekly. 'I didn't realise things were getting so bad,' he mumbled.

'Didn't realise! Didn't realise! Good heavens boy, you've got eyes in your head haven't you? Look around at the dust, the decay, the untidiness. This place is more like a wretched mausoleum now than a house.'

Jonas stared at his napkin.

'What on earth are you going to do?'

There was a long pause and the only sound in the room was the faint hissing of the logs on the dying fire.

'I was … I was hoping that perhaps … Well, perhaps you might help me, Aunt.'

'Help you.'

'If you could see some way to letting me have some money ...'

Aunt Emilia emitted a cry that seemed to be a strange combination of a scream and an ejaculation of rage.

'So that's it, is it? You want me to help fund your profligate ways. To shore up your incompetence with my money. Having squandered your parents' fortune, you now seek to squander mine.'

Her voice was loud and harsh and reverberated around the large chamber.

'I was hoping ...'

'Well, hope again, boy. Not one penny of mine will I pass to you while I am alive. I suspected that I would be presented with this bare-faced entreaty when you encouraged me to visit you earlier than my usual time. You always were transparent.' She threw down her napkin and rose unsteadily to her feet. 'To say that you have disappointed me would be a great understatement. Your profligacy has sullied your parents' memory, which I find unforgiveable. I am ashamed to call you kin. I bid you good night.'

With these words echoing around the barren dining room, Aunt Emilia departed, slamming the door on her exit. Reaching the foot of the stairs, she paused, leaning against the wall. Her heart was pumping wildly and she felt faint. The doctor had advised her to avoid any form of over excitement. Her fragile heart was not strong enough to cope with strong passions and here she was allowing her fury at her nephew's ruthless indolence to boil over. She couldn't help it. His selfish indulgences and excesses had been eating away at her for some time and when the brat appealed to her for money to continue in the same fashion … Well! This thought sent another spasm of pain to her chest. She must take her pills. She had left them in her room. She knew they would help control the erratic rhythm of her heart, which was already causing her severe discomfort. In truth, she knew that it was the pills that were keeping her alive. Taking a deep breath, she mounted the stairs and made her way slowly to her bedroom.

Lighting the candles, she moved to the table by the window where she had left her pillbox. It wasn't there, but its absence was not the reason that she gasped and clutched her chest. It was the presence on the table of that wretched skull she had demanded Jonas remove from the room. It gleamed eerily in the flickering light and seemed to be grinning at her. But what caused Aunt Emilia to sink to her knees with fear and horror was the sight of the blood that was dripping from the eye sockets, leaving spidery red traces down the side of the skull.

The fierce pain in her chest now seemed to consume her whole body. Those red, blood-soaked eyes seemed to glower in triumph at her. They were a portent of death: her death. They were willing her heart to stop. Her torso twisted in agony and then with a final groan, she fell forward on her face. She was quite dead.

It was some thirty minutes later when the door opened and a figure entered the room. It was Jonas Blackstock. He stared down at the lifeless form of his aunt, his features registering no emotion whatsoever and then suddenly he smiled; this progressed into a chuckle and then a hearty laugh.

'Good night, sweet aunt,' he intoned when his laughter had subsided, 'a flight angels sing thee to thy rest.' This brought on another bout of laughter.

Then he moved to the table by the window and lifted up the skull and stroked it, before inserting his finger into one of the eye sockets. He removed it and lifted the now crimson digit up towards the candlelight, his eyes sparkling with merriment. 'Red ink,' he said quietly. 'My dear aunt, it was only red ink.'

By early spring, the business concerning his aunt's will had been settled and Jonas Blackstock had been left a considerable portion of her fortune. He had already started to make inroads into the funds through an expensive sojourn to London where he had purchased costly volumes and trinkets to enhance his studies into the black arts. He returned to Brookfield Hall on 21st March, the spring equinox, the date, in fact, when his aunt had been due to visit again. In recognition of this, he toasted her heartily with a fine bottle of Burgundy which he supped with his dinner that evening. Somewhat unsteadily, he made his way early to his bedchamber and it was only while he was disrobing that he noticed the skull. The stigmata skull. It was sitting on his dressing table. He had no idea how it had got there. It certainly was none of his doing. He had left it in his aunt's room.

His body tingling with apprehension, he approached the skull cautiously and then took a step back in horror. Blood was seeping from its eyes and trickling down its bony visage. It was blood this time, he knew. Rich, thick blood. He attempted to cry out but his throat constricted with the dread that assailed him, and all that emerged from his open mouth was a strange strangulated croak. He was held frozen by the sight of the skull and the shimmering scarlet effusion that drooled from its eye sockets.

And then he heard a strange rustling from behind him. Slowly he willed his body to turn in the direction of the sound. Standing before him was the figure of Aunt Emilia. It was as though he was viewing her reflection in an ancient pitted mirror, a colourless, wavering image. She smiled at Jonas and raised her hand in greeting.

'I have arrived for my spring visit.'

He heard the words in his head. The voice was that of his aunt's but she had not opened her mouth.

He croaked the same cry of terror once more, twisting his head back to gaze at the skull again. Now, it was completely covered in blood. A seething crimson entity vibrating with evil.

And he knew; he knew what this meant.

He wanted to move, he wanted to run, but he was transfixed by the horrid thing before him. Slowly he felt the energy dissipate from his body as though some invisible force was switching off all his organs. He crumpled to the floor. As he lay there, life ebbing away from him, splatters of blood from the stigmata skull dripped down upon his face.

14

THE CHRISTMAS ANGEL

Miss Skilbeck placed the wooden stool by the side of the Christmas tree and, with a nimbleness that belied her sixty years, clambered up on to it. As the ancient stool creaked in protest, she reached up to the top of the tree, leaning into its feathery branches that smelt so pleasingly of pine. With great precision she fixed the cardboard angel to the green spiny spire with a fine needle.

'Poor thing. That angel has seen better days,' she observed, returning once more to terra firma.

The Reverend Thomas Wolpert looked up from the dusty prayer book he was perusing, the amber light from the altar candles catching the pebble lenses of his spectacles and setting them aglow. 'We both have, Miss Skilbeck, that angel and I,' he sniffed, 'yet I believe we are good for a few years yet.'

In response to this barbed reply, Miss Skilbeck flushed and announced her own warm feelings on the matter. 'It's a great shame to display such a shabby trinket for the children to see. It hardly represents the image of the angel Gabriel who appeared to the shepherds watching over their sheep. No glory will shine all around from that grubby antique relic.

Surely we can purchase another one. A few shillings is all that is needed.'

The Reverend Wolpert closed his book with some force, the sound echoing through the empty church. 'A few shillings are more than I am prepared to spare,' he said in a voice that was low but edged with steel. 'That angel has looked down on several generations of children without having any ill effect upon them. It will suffice, I say. What care I for fair weather worshippers anyway? Why should I fork out good money to provide a new spangled angel for them to gawp at? Too much money is wasted on children at this time of the year as it is.' He paused briefly, lifting his thick lens towards the top of the tree. 'That fairy stays.'

Miss Skilbeck sighed. The old skinflint, she thought. At this Christian time of kindness to all men, how could he begrudge a few coins if it gladdened the hearts of the youngsters who filled the church over Christmas? Mr Penny Pincher! He kept the church like an icebox rather than spending a little more on the heating to make it comfortable for those who came here to worship. She cast a searching glance at Reverend Wolpert, a skeleton of a man with white hair, pinched cheeks and an avaricious gleam in his eyes, trapped behind the convex wall of his spectacles. Taking up the stool, she went back to the vestry without another word. She determined to fund this so-called extravagance herself. She would purchase a new golden angel from the toyshop in the village and throw the tattered relic in the dustbin.

She emerged a few moments later in a thick tweed coat and a large woolly hat.

'Going already?' intoned the cleric, hardly glancing in her direction, his nose once more in the ancient prayer book.

'Yes, I've got my father's tea to see to,' she replied starchily.

'Ah, yes, well please remember to remind Farmer Thornton about the holly boughs for the church ledges. He's late bringing them this year.'

'I will. Good night.'

It snowed that night and Reverend Thomas Wolpert woke to find white spears of frosty light playing on the ceiling of his bedroom: a winter kaleidoscope. As he hurried to the church, he noticed that there had been a visitor already. The smooth white snow on the churchyard path was marked by a single set of footprints. Once inside, and feeling not much warmer, he observed the wet prints leading up the aisle towards the altar. Here they veered off to the right, past the pulpit and ending by the Christmas tree. Turning the corner by the top pew, he came upon a sight which caused him to groan and stagger towards the altar rail. There, lying at the foot of the tree, her head resting in a pool of blood, was Miss Skilbeck. Clutched in her hand was a shiny new Christmas angel.

When the police arrived, along with the village doctor, it was assumed that Miss Skilbeck had overreached herself while trying to place the new angel on the top of the tree. She had fallen off the stool, cracking her head on the corner of a pew as she did so. The unfortunate incident was recorded as death by misadventure.

That evening the Reverend Wolpert sat by his meagre fire shivering, not so much with cold as with remorse. Staring into the feeble flames which struggled vainly to flicker with some warmth, he fancied he saw in their darting yellow tongues the shape of a golden angel. There could be no doubt about it: there were the wings, the halo ... He was mesmerised by the image, but his heart gave a jolt when he observed the shape move. Slowly it fluttered closer to the edge of the grate. He was sure of it. Now, it stood on the soot-blackened bar, its head raised towards his, its tiny eyes fierce and resentful.

The Reverend Wolpert gave a little groan and quickly reached for the poker. He must stir up the fire and rid himself of this hallucination. But as his hand clasped the cold iron handle of the poker, the angel rose from the fire and flew into the air. Wolpert gave a scream, dropping the poker and flinging himself back in his chair with a moan of terror. He could not take his eyes from this fantastic apparition which now seemed to be growing in size. He began to sob and in a frantic attempt to rid himself of this nightmare vision, he screwed his eyes shut.

Eventually, when he dared open them again, the vision had disappeared. The fire burned feebly as before and no diabolical mannequin hovered before him. And yet ... and yet there was a strange iridescent glow in the darkness of the room – a glow that seemed to be coming from behind him and throwing weird shadows into the chimney breast. With a dry mouth and shaking body, the Reverend Wolpert summoned what courage he had in his frosty old heart and turned around.

Suddenly the whole room was filled with a fierce amber light, at the centre of which was the angel, now some six feet in height. She was gazing at him with a heart-stopping intensity. Gazing, he thought, into his very soul and the sins of miserliness that were lodged there. The aged cleric fell to his knees. Simple, childlike words escaped from his parched throat. 'Please forgive me, I'm sorry.' No sooner had the words been spoken than an overpowering weakness coursed through his frame and a grey mist thickened before his eyes into a dense black curtain of unconsciousness. Slowly, the Reverend Wolpert's body slumped to the floor.

The clergyman woke to find himself in his own bed. He sat up, rubbed his eyes and gazed around him: all was normal. It had been a dream. Just a bad dream. Thank the Lord. He lay back on his pillow, relieved and yet not content. He gazed up at the ceiling and observed fine spears of frosty light playing there: a winter kaleidoscope. It had snowed in the night again.

That morning, the morning of Christmas Eve, Reverend Wolpert hurried to the village toyshop bright and early. He was their first customer and not only bought a new angel for the tree, but also a collection of bright new baubles and shiny ornaments. He was determined that this year the tree would look the best it had ever done.

As he hurried to the church he noticed that there had been a visitor already: the smooth white snow on the churchyard path was marked with a single set of footprints. Once inside, and not feeling much warmer, he observed footprints leading up the aisle to the altar. The icy chill of fear began to seep into his veins. He knew … he knew these were the same footprints as before.

Slowly, reluctantly, he began to make his way up the aisle, following the damp trail on the floor. As he neared the altar, he heard something faint but distinctive on the musty air of the old church. It was humming: the gentle, pleasant humming of a Christmas carol.

He turned the corner by the top pew and met a sight which caused him to drop his package of ornaments. Standing on tiptoe on a rickety stool was Miss Skilbeck. She was reaching up to place a new shiny angel on the top of the Christmas tree. She turned in surprise at seeing the Reverend Wolpert and lost her balance, the stool giving way under her. As she began to fall, some force propelled the cleric forward, arms outstretched. She fell awkwardly into his embrace.

'Ooh,' she cried, catching her breath, and disentangling herself. 'You gave me a real shock there.'

'Are you all right?' the Reverend Wolpert asked with some difficultly.

'Nothing a nice cup of tea won't cure,' she smiled.

'I … I er … took your advice, Miss Skilbeck. I have purchased a new angel for the tree and a few other little decorations.' He moved to retrieve the package from where he had dropped it while Miss Skilbeck stared at him open-mouthed.

'Perhaps you'd like to make that cup of tea, while I decorate the tree. I think we both could do with a hot drink,' he continued.

'Yes, of course.'

As she turned to go, she found the old cleric's hand on hers. 'I … I really am most sorry for being … for being so poor in spirit, Miss Skilbeck. You'll find that I will be somewhat different in the future.' His features softened, the frost melting. 'I hope you can forgive me.'

'Of course. Of course I can,' she said gently, returning the smile. 'After all it is the season of good will.'

For a moment neither of them said anything and then the Reverend Wolpert patted her arm. 'Now, that tea,' he said, 'and turn the central heating up a notch while you're at it as well, eh. It's a bit too chilly in here.'

Miss Skilbeck gave a cheerful nod and bustled off to the vestry. Slowly and uneasily at first, the Reverend Wolpert began to redecorate the tree, replacing the old and tired trimmings with the shiny new ones. Finally, he removed the tissue wrapping from the splendid new angel. He held it tremulously and gazed at the glowing trinket – the spangled cardboard, the tinselled halo and the plastic features which, for a brief moment, seemed real. The eyes appeared to twinkle and the mouth to smile. But strangely he felt no fear or apprehension, no concern at all, only an easing of the spirit.

Some moments later Miss Skilbeck returned with the tea. 'After I've drunk this,' she said, 'I'll get on with cleaning the church. We want it to look really nice on Christmas Day. The floor is in a bit of a mess. Have you seen this mark here? She pointed to a stain by the corner of the top pew. 'If I didn't know better, I'd say it was blood.'

15

INSTANT
REMOVALS

To some extent, Ralph Beaton was oblivious of the early morning rush. He was driving on automatic pilot. He had a lot on his mind and his brows furrowed as he contemplated his lot. In fact he had not been really happy for at least three months – ever since that faceless foreign corporation, International Essentials, had taken over the thriving local firm he worked for. It was not just that he had changed from being a medium-sized cog in a cosy machine to a very small one in a clinical, anonymous conglomeration. No, that was not all: in some indefinable way, he also felt threatened.

The familiar management had virtually disappeared overnight, pensioned or promoted elsewhere, he assumed, and they had been replaced by tight-lipped, blank-faced, dark-suited individuals with nondescript faces. Individuals? Well, no, that was it: they were not individuals. They were blanks. In personality and appearance they were identical.

His closest colleagues had also left the company without a word. Even his best friend had moved on without telling him – transferred to one of the overseas branches, the management had informed him – but no forwarding address had been made available. And now, Ralph felt the pressure on himself to leave. Nothing had been said openly to him. He just sensed it: International Essentials wanted their own men.

Ralph pulled up sharply at the roundabout as the furniture van in front braked prematurely. The jolt brought his mind back to his driving. Dangerous, he thought, losing concentration on a busy road like this.

The furniture van was open at the back and in the gloom of the interior, he glimpsed items of furniture, cunningly arranged in a neat and compact fashion: the mainstay and fabric of someone's home on the move. Ralph gave a wry grin. How easily they were whisked away.

As the van pulled forward, what appeared to be a roll of carpet, which had been propped against an old sideboard, suddenly slumped sideways and leaned at an awkward angle near the tailboard. But, as Ralph followed the van around the roundabout, he came to realise that it wasn't a roll of carpet after all.

It was a body.

Needles of shock pierced the back of his neck and his mouth gaped open. Surely, he was imagining it. His eyes were playing tricks on him. But no. As he drew nearer to the van, staring hard into its dim interior, he could make out the body's shape and features. It was a middle-aged man, balding, with a scarlet wound on the top of his head. Ralph's mind reeled. What on earth was going on?

Now, on the straight road again, the furniture van began to surge forward. Automatically, Ralph put his foot down. He had to get to the bottom of this strange business.

Mentally, he made a note of the number plate. RIP 4321. RIP 4321. He repeated the number to himself.

Despite the speed of Ralph's car, the van gradually began to pull ahead; and then, suddenly, with only with the briefest flash of its indicator light, it turned a sharp right on to a side road. Ralph saw the body swing back against the sideboard into its original position, the head lolling in a broken-necked fashion in the shadows. An on-coming lorry blared its horn and flashed its lights as the furniture van shot across its path.

As the van began to disappear up the side road, Ralph caught sight of the firm's name, painted in bold, black lettering: Instant Removals. He waited, impatiently, biting his lip, unable to turn because of the continuous stream of oncoming traffic. When at last he was able to move, he roared at great speed down the leafy side road, but there was no sign of the van.

'I wish to report a murder.'

The stoical expression on the desk sergeant's face did not change. Murder, rape, assassination, you name it, I've seen it all, the craggy features and tired eyes seemed to say.

'Oh yes, sir?' he responded after a measured pause.

'Yes. I've just seen a dead body.'

'Really.' The tone was laconic, unruffled. Ralph might just as well have been reporting a missing dog. 'Where was this, sir?'

'In a furniture van.' Ralph was fully aware how stupid this sounded.

'In a furniture van,' the policeman repeated slowly, his face immobile.

'Let me explain.'

'Please do.' The sergeant leaned forward on the counter, cupping his face in his hands.

Ralph told him the story.

'I see,' said the policeman with a weary sigh when he'd finished. He was visibly unimpressed.

'I know how it sounds, but it's the truth. I swear it,' said Ralph with some passion.

'What was the name and number plate again?'

'Instant Removals. RIP 4321.'

The sergeant jotted down the information on his notepad, with exquisite slowness, licking the tip of his pencil every few letters. 'Now sir,' he said at length, 'if you'll just take a seat, I'll see what our computer can dig up for us. I'll just be a little while. There's a coffee machine around the corner, if you'd like a drink. It's not very nice, though.' With these words of comfort he disappeared through the swing doors behind him.

Half an hour went by before the desk sergeant returned. He shook his head before he spoke. 'I'm afraid we can't help you, sir. The information you gave us has drawn a blank.'

'What?'

'There's no trace of a firm with the name Instant Removals and no vehicle with the registration you gave me.'

'But that's impossible ...' Ralph realised his voice was unnaturally loud.

The policeman narrowed his eyes. 'Are you sure you're all right, sir? You seem to be rather overexcited.'

'Of course I'm all right. I'm just concerned that you don't seem to believe me. You think I've imagined the whole thing, don't you?'

'It's not really a case of whether I believe you or not, sir. But ERIC doesn't.'

Who's Eric?'

'Our computer. Electronic Retrieval of Information Console. He's infallible. Marvellous things, computers. They'll replace us all one day.'

Ralph could hardly believe what he was hearing. His face flushed with anger. 'So, because your computer can't come up with anything on the facts I've given you, you're not going to do anything about it.'

'Well, there's not a lot we can do, sir. Not on the information you've provided.'

'But a man's been murdered!'

'So you say.'

'What's that supposed to mean?'

The policeman tried to adopt a more conciliatory tone. 'Now, sir, you admitted yourself that at first you thought this "body" was just a roll of carpet. Perhaps …'

'It was a body! I'm certain of it. And the name was Instant Removals. And the registration was RIP 4321.'

The policeman smiled and nodded good-humouredly, the way he might when dealing with an imbecile. 'I have made a note of that information. If you'd like to make a statement, we might be able to follow this up at a later date'.

Ralph drew away from the police station in a rage. What a farce! Probably they would shove his statement in a drawer somewhere and forget all about it. It was quite obvious that the sergeant had thought he'd escaped from somewhere. Bodies in the back of removal vans? Take more water with it next time, eh? Well, he supposed, it did sound fantastic, but he was in no doubt as to what he'd seen. For a fleeting moment, the image of the grey-faced corpse flashed into his mind and he winced. He consoled himself with the thought that he had done all he could about it. If the police and bloody ERIC didn't believe him, it wasn't his fault.

He glanced at the clock on the dashboard. It was just after twelve. The morning was gone and if the police wouldn't believe what had happened, what chance was there that his new superior at International Essentials would.

But his mouth was dry; he needed a drink. There was quite a decent pub not far from the factory. Ralph decided to call in for a quick pint before facing the music about his late arrival.

Ten minutes later, he pulled up at The Fox and Grapes. He was just locking his car when he saw it. The furniture van. The Instant Removals van. It was parked close to the pub's entrance. He ran over to it and peered into the back. It was empty: no furniture, no roll of carpet, no body. He looked around him to see if he was being watched, but the car park was quiet and there was no one in sight. He checked the number plate and felt a thrill of excitement as he read it: RIP 4321.

'I knew I was right. I knew I was bloody well right,' he crowed in a fierce whisper.

Suddenly, he heard a noise. A couple of teenage lads tumbled out of the pub, laughing and pushing each other about. With affected nonchalance, Ralph strolled back to his own car. Here, he was determined to wait. This time he'd make sure he didn't lose them. He'd get to the bottom of this business, if it was the last thing he did.

After about half an hour, two burly characters strolled out of The Fox and Grapes and approached the van. They were dressed in grey overalls with red badges, very similar, Ralph thought, to those worn by the workforce of International Essentials.

When the van pulled out of the car park, Ralph was right behind it. No way were they going to get away from him this time. As it happened, it moved at a more leisurely pace, keeping well within the speed limit. To Ralph's surprise, he found himself retracing the route of his morning journey. As he followed the van up increasingly familiar roads, he felt a gnawing sickness in his stomach. It was when the van finally stopped, that he froze with horror.

They had drawn up outside his own house.

16

THE
BOOKS

I have a story to tell, and for my own peace of mind, I must tell it. I am a bibliophile of some note, well known amongst that circle of experts whose business it is to be cognisant of such things. Great and rare books have found their way into my possession without my ever having to advertise myself abroad. Word of mouth is most potent for those in search of the knowledge. So it was that Aubrey Fleming stepped into my shop some twenty years ago. (Shop I call it, but really it consists of the book-filled rooms which are my home).

Fleming was a tall, gaunt man with white wispy hair which had the appearance of never having been touched by comb or brush. From deep within the hollow sockets of his face there sparkled the darkest eyes I have ever seen. He came to call without an appointment on a bleak November day. It was not yet noon, but already my oil lamp was lit. I was poring over some ancient tome that had come into my possession, a work of religious perversion penned by Italian monks in the fifteenth century, when I found Fleming at my side. He had entered so silently that I was quite taken aback by his presence. He apologised for the obvious shock he had given me and then quickly launched into an explanation for his visit.

Apparently his brother, Ambrose, a retired missionary, had just passed away leaving Aubrey as executor to deal with his estate, the bulk of which was a crumbling old ruin, Mullhaven Lodge. The said domicile, Aubrey informed me, was crammed to the roof with books. Apparently Ambrose, in his missionary travels, had collected books with as much zeal as he exerted in attempting to convert the natives.

'I have neither interest nor expertise in this area,' observed the gaunt Aubrey Fleming, his voice emerging as a rasping whisper, 'that is why I have sought you out. I am sure you will find volumes of unique quality in my brother's collection. If you will agree to catalogue it, I am sure we can come to some agreeable financial arrangement.'

I have reached my position as a highly regarded bibliophile through a natural love of and curiosity for books. I could not resist an opportunity such as the one presented to me now. Therefore it was agreed that the following day I would travel down to Mullhaven Lodge, which stood near the coast on the Essex marshes, and spend a week there cataloguing the books. It seemed to me at the time, a most pleasant way to take a brief holiday and if one or two of the rarer volumes found their way into my luggage on my return, surely it was only a fair bonus for my time and trouble.

Mullhaven Lodge turned out to be as bleak and crumbling as I had imagined. It was a solitary protuberance on the flat, misty marshes. Its only visible neighbours were just a few hardy trees, gnarled and twisted by the fierce salty winds from the sea. Aubrey Fleming, who was to have met me at the small village station, failed to appear and I had to hire a pony and trap to take me to the Lodge. The driver, an unshaven, taciturn man, was reluctant to convey me out there and only an increase in coin persuaded him. As I expected, he proved poor company on that miserable journey. He rarely responded to my comments and questions and when he did deign to do so it was with an unintelligible grunt.

I was dumped unceremoniously at the end of the winding path leading to the Lodge and, with a fierce clatter of hooves, the trap turned around and raced back down the narrow road. Soon it was only a shimmering silhouette merging into the rising mist.

Pulling my coat about me, I made my way up the path towards the house. No light flickered behind those dark panes and an uneasy though struck me: was I on a fool's errand? If Aubrey Fleming was not waiting for me inside, what was I to do? Night was falling fast and I was stranded out here with no means of returning to the village. An unfocused anger began to well up within me.

With growing irritation, I pounded on the large ring knocker on the sturdy front door. I heard the sound booming like distant cannon fire into the gloomy recesses of the house. I waited some while but there was no response. My heart sank. It was as I had feared. I had been lured to this God-forsaken place by some lunatic – for what purpose I could not fathom. I tried the handle of the door and, to my great surprise, it turned easily and the door swung open.

I found myself in a dank musty hallway at the far end of which a door stood slightly ajar. From the room there came a strange yellow glow which sent fine rippling splinters of light on to the floor of the hallway. Glancing over my shoulder at the onset of the inhospitable night, I knew there was little option for me but to investigate the source of this light and, on entering the room, I found, to my delight, a hearty fire flickering in the grate. On a table in the centre of the room were an unlit oil lamp, a carafe of wine, glasses and a large silver dish-cover to which a note was attached. I lit the lamp which, while bathing the room in a dismal amber gloom, was much preferable to the eerie firelight. The note was from Aubrey Fleming. It read:

My Dear Sir,

I must apologise profusely for not meeting you from your train. Unfortunately, circumstances beyond my control prevented me from doing so. However, I shall attend on you within the next twenty-four hours. In the meantime, a bed has been aired for you in the room directly at the top of the stairs and I have left a cold supper under this cover. The books – they are all around you.

Aubrey Fleming.

I found my mind more at ease. Throwing off my coat, I poured myself a glass of wine and spent some moments perusing the shelves which covered three walls of the room. There were titles here which I had never dreamed of seeing – rarities which were priceless. On taking a few down, I experienced that familiar frisson of pleasure as my hands held the cool, finely tooled leather and felt the expert binding. I opened the books and let the pages ripple gently through my fingers.

Their condition was immaculate; it was as though no other man had handled them. I was in Aladdin's cave.

Despite my somewhat gloomy surroundings, all my irritations were now dispelled. Beaming joyfully, I replenished my glass and toasted my own good fortune. Suddenly I felt hungry. The cold wine on my empty stomach must have sharpened my appetite. Fleming had left me a cold supper – why not eat it now?

I had no premonition of the sight which was to greet me as I eagerly raised the silver dish-cover. Beneath it was a plate which contained what must have been a chicken salad, but it was difficult to determine the exact nature of the meal for the plate was rippling with motion as though it was alive. Indeed, it was alive – the foul mound pulsated with the obscene wriggling bodies of fat yellow maggots, a mass of them, gorging on the rancid meat. This gruesome vision was accompanied by an overpowering fetid reek which assailed my nostrils.

Clamping the dish-cover back over the disgusting feast, I staggered back into one of the chairs, my heart pounding against my ribs. This whole visit was now taking on the dimensions of a waking nightmare. Was this some kind of ghastly jest? I did not know and I did not care. My addled brain, far from seeking an explanation, sought an escape. Glancing back at the innocent-seeming dish-cover, I felt I could almost hear the foul creatures writhing beneath its shiny exterior. I have a singular abhorrence of such creatures and my feelings of revulsion were so strong I knew I could remain in that room no longer. Logic, and a further glass of wine (to steady my nerves), told me that the only sensible course of action was to retire to the bedroom prepared for me and depart this dreadful place at the earliest light.

With some trepidation, and a further glass of wine, I took the oil lamp and made my way up the stairs to the chamber where I was to spend the night. To my surprise and relief, the room was pleasantly appointed, and although no fire crackled in the grate, a reasonably warm bottle was nestling under the sheets. By the time I was snug beside it, my unease and fearful apprehensions were fading. I had overreacted, I thought, to nothing more than a case of bad housekeeping. I dozed fitfully for some time, but real sleep failed to visit me. My mind could not rest, always returning, after several diversions of thought, to the treasure house of ancient tomes which lay below my sleeping quarters. My love of books (some might say my greed) would not allow me to sleep. Mustering my courage, I determined to disregard that mass of foul creatures beneath the dish-cover and to investigate the shelves below, taking a few of the choicest items and slipping them into my luggage before making my escape as compensation for the discomfort and indignity I had endured.

As I was about to leave the warm confines of the bed, a noise, a faint, scraping noise came to my ears, holding me fast. In the darkness, I pulled myself up in the bed and listened, my ears straining to determine the cause of the sound. It came again, regular, insistent, resolute and growing louder, like the Devil's whisper. It was as though some thing was scraping its way up the stairs, towards the bedroom.

For a moment the noise ceased, as though the thing, whatever it might be, was resting on the stair. I waited, hardly daring to breathe. Perhaps it was all in my mind. If the noise did not come again in a minute, then I would know I had imagined it.

Too many glasses of wine. That was it. The alcohol had stimulated my imagination. I waited, my eyes staring into the blackness of the bedroom, only being able to discern the faint outline of the door on the far wall. The silence hissed in my ears.

Nothing.

I began to relax. I had been right: it was just a trick my over-active mind had been playing on me. There really was nothing to be concerned about.

And then it came again, louder, closer. But this time the scraping noise was accompanied by another sound: a shrill, tortured wheezing as that of an asthmatic or dying man.

I was gripped by an uncontrollable urge to scream, my mouth falling open in anticipation of this expression of horror and fear, but I stayed silent, as though some invisible hand were at my throat, squeezing, holding the cry back. I knew, to my increasing terror, that whatever creature was making this fearful noise was now outside the room. I heard it fumble for the handle, its weight bumping against the door.

I could not move. I could not speak. I could only stare in terror as the door of the room began to swing slowly open.

To recall that moment even now makes my blood run cold. I had often heard of the expression, never really believing in the reality of such an experience, but now as I recall that night long ago, the fierce chill of fear once again begins to seep into my veins.

As the door opened, a broad shaft of moonlight from the window on the landing spilled into the room, backlighting the apparition which stood in the doorway. It was a man – or at least the remains of a man. A skeleton with flesh, with the remnants of some loose garment hanging in tatters about its slight frame. It stood in the crouched and twisted stance of a cripple, and indeed the thing was missing one of its arms. The face, thank God, was in shadow, but the eyes glittered fiercely in the gloom.

The sound of its hoarse wheezing filled the room, grating in my mind like the pumping of an enormous bellows. For a moment it remained still, like some grotesque statue, and then, with its right leg scraping along the ground, the creature shuffled forward, holding its arm out in a gesture of supplication. At that moment, whatever force had been holding my scream in check released me, and I cried out in terror and panic before collapsing back on my pillow in a dead faint.

When I awoke, the shifting grey shadows of morning were filtering into the room. For some moments I lay, cold and somewhat dazed, gazing at the ceiling, trying to remember where I was until, with frightening clarity, the whole ghastly experience came back to me. I quickly sat up and glanced around the gloomy room, but there was no sign of my night-time visitor and no indication that anyone or anything had visited the chamber, except that the door was still ajar. I scrambled into my clothes and made my way downstairs. I was just heading for the front door when my steps began to falter. As I passed the book room I remembered all those precious volumes sitting there on the shelves, neatly, temptingly. There were some rarities I would probably never see again. Despite my fear, despite my need to leave that dreadful house, I could not resist another look.

Everything was as I had left it the night before, with the faint beams of the early morning sun spotlighting the dish-cover. I shuddered at the memory of its disgusting contents but then my eyes lighted on the shelves lining the room and all other emotions were subsumed in my overwhelming passion for books.

In about twenty minutes I had scrutinised the shelves. As my eyes ran over the scores of wonderful titles, I frantically tried to decide which ones to choose. Eventually, I withdrew four of the choicest tomes and proceeded to stuff them in my travelling bag. Small payment indeed, I thought, for my ordeal. I was just buckling up my bag when I became conscious of a shadow falling across my face. With jumping nerves I glanced up and saw Aubrey Fleming staring down at me.

'Not leaving?' he asked in his strange hoarse voice.

'Yes,' I said tersely, wondering how long he had been standing there, watching me.

'I am so terribly sorry not to have been here yesterday, but I was unavoidably detained in town.' He hesitated and frowned as though he had great difficulty in phrasing his next question.

'I hope … I hope everything has been all right for you?'

'No,' I replied sharply, 'everything has not been all right for me.' And yet as I spoke, I realised how foolish my story would sound in the cold light of a new day – the ramblings of a man who had had too much to drink the night before. Instinctively, I glanced over to where the jug of wine stood: it was empty. I now hesitated to mention even the supper I'd been left in case that turned out to be some drink-induced hallucination.

'You have been disturbed?' Fleming said quietly, his ashen face perhaps betraying more than the simple question revealed.

'Too disturbed to stay here any longer. I am afraid I cannot accept your commission, Mr Fleming. I intend to leave immediately.'

I grabbed my bag, considerably heavier now with its contraband, and made for the door. Fleming's skeletal hand caught my sleeve and for a moment he held me with his dark gaze.

'Let me at least accompany you to the village.'

'No, no, that will not be necessary,' I cried, pulling myself away from him and rushing out of the room and the house.

I remember little of my flight down the long, lonely road towards the village. I do know I kept glancing behind, expecting to see Fleming chasing after me; but all I observed was the pale grey sky and the stark, phantom trees piercing the morning mist. I knew that as long as the books were on my person I was a guilty man. Once in London I would be safe; it would then be easy to deny all knowledge of the missing volumes.

On reaching the outskirts of the village I espied the driver of the pony and trap who had taken me out to Mullhaven Lodge the day before. Now nearly exhausted, I was thankful of my luck and I hailed him. He was, I could tell, somewhat surprised to see me, but when I thrust some coins in his hand, begging that he convey me to the station, he readily agreed.

'You got on all right at the Lodge?' he said in his dour taciturn way when I had climbed aboard the trap.

'Yes,' I replied. 'What do you know of the place?'

He gave me a sharp glance. 'Nothing. Nothing that I shouldn't. I know it's been empty some time now.'

'Since Ambrose Fleming's death.'

He nodded. 'And what a death.'

'Why, what happened?'

The driver screwed up his face and whipped up the reins 'He was a missionary, y'know.'

'Yes.'

'Playing with fire, if you ask me: goin' into those heathen countries. An African tribe, it was, who turned on him – tortured him. Before killing him, they cut off one of his arms and ate it in front of the poor devil. So the story goes.'

I felt my stomach turn to lead at these words. Despite the coldness of the day, I suddenly began to perspire profusely. 'It … it must have been a great blow to his brother.'

The driver gave a strange, twisted, cheerless grin. 'It certainly was. At the news of his brother's death, Aubrey Fleming dropped dead of a heart attack.'

On the train back to London, I took the four volumes that I had acquired from the library at Mullhaven Lodge and cast them out of the carriage window.

17

THE OLDEST GHOST-STORY WRITER IN THE LAND

I t was remarkable, thought Montague Dane as he sipped his tea cautiously, that Grant's Hotel had managed to retain so much of its period charm in these ravaged times. With a little persuasive imagination one could almost feel one-self back in those heady pre-war days when the Ghost Club writers would meet each month to spin one another ghoulish yarns. The gatherings were ego trips for second-rate authors of course, but nonetheless highly pleasurable.

The hot sweet tea caught the back of his throat and he gave a sharp intake of breath. With a slightly shaking hand, he replaced the cup in the saucer. His parchment features creased into a wistful smile. The Ghost Club. Ah, well, they were all ghosts themselves now – all, that is, except himself: the oldest ghost-story writer in the land. Although, he had to admit, it was some years since he'd actually written anything, apart from the odd letter to the local paper com-plaining about the drains or the erratic refuse collection in his area. It was strange how the desire to create, to surprise, to chill, had left him. One of the penalties of growing old, he supposed.

He risked another mouthful of tea. At least he had thought the desire to tell a story had gone, until that very morning when he'd caught the train up to town. Something he'd seen had caused a faint phantom of an idea to lodge itself in his brain and he'd experienced the long-forgotten urge to write it down. He stared over at the regular bluish gas flame of the fire in the lounge of Grant's Hotel and let his mind wander to the little story of the lost boy on the darkened station.

'Mr Dane?'

Like the shattering of a mirror, the picture broke into myriad splintered pieces in his mind.

He turned to look at the speaker. She was a young, dark-haired woman with a very pale complexion and vivid red lips. They parted to reveal an arctic waste of teeth.

'Mr Dane,' she repeated, the smile broadening.

He gave a stately nod of the head.

'I'm Shara Lewis from City Television. Sorry I'm late. Traffic.' Her grey eyes rolled ceiling-ward.

She pulled up a chair and gave a peremptory wave to a passing flunkey. A lady who is used to getting her own way, Dane thought.

After ordering herself a black coffee, she turned to face him, still beaming. It was a pretty face, or it could have been, but it was somehow clinical, swept clean of character by the pale make-up, red lips and heavy eyeliner. It was almost like look-ing into the face of a shop-window mannequin.

'It's such a thrill to meet you, Mr Dane. I have been a great fan of yours since my school days. I used to read your stories under the bedclothes in my dormitory at night and nearly frightened myself to death.' She giggled. 'I couldn't sleep for nights after reading "The Whisperings".'

Some of the titles meant nothing to him now. They were like fragments from another life. However, 'The Whisperings' did remain with him; it was his most anthologised work. A tale of ghostly whisperings that told of deeds not in the past, as the central character in the story had thought, but of the future.

'Which story are you dramatising tonight?' Dane asked, as the girl accepted the coffee from the waiter, her short black skirt riding up to show what the writer considered to be an indecent expanse of leg.

'"The Withered Rose". I think they've done a super job on it. Very atmospheric. Damien Tinker is playing the young curate.'

He was unfamiliar with both story and actor, but he smiled indulgently.

'What are you writing at the moment?' she asked, before sipping her coffee with a practised elegance.

He looked beyond her to far side of the lounge. Something had caught his attention. Were his old eyes deceiving him or was that the boy he'd seen on the platform that morning? Small, pale, with large liquid eyes and a haunted expression. He stood alone in the corner of the room as though he'd been left there and forgotten. There was something strangely familiar about the urchin, for such he was. The heat of the room swirled a transparent haze around the boy and he seemed almost to be floating. Slowly he turned his gaze towards Dane and their eyes met. The author felt himself grow cold. An unknown and irrational fear had crept upon him and was now gripping him. It was a very different sensation to the cosy manufactured chills he'd experienced in the old days when the Ghost Club used to meet here. This was real and all the more terrifying because he didn't know why he was frightened. For a moment, his body turned to ice and his heart began to race. He blinked furiously, gasping for breath.

'Are you all right?' Shara Lewis touched him on the shoulder. 'Mr Dane.' He felt limp, the panic disappearing as quickly as it came. The girl's face swam before his eyes, blearily at first and then it moved crisply into focus.

'I'm sorry,' he said, his words slurring somewhat.

'Are you feeling OK?'

'Yes, yes, my dear. I'm fine,' he said, attempting to reassure her. 'What were you saying?'

'I was just wondering what you were writing at the present?' she said, awkwardly, wondering if this old guy was going to make it to the transmission that evening. They should have filmed his slot rather than attempt to do it live. But that was Gavin for you.

'Writing? Well, I haven't actually written a new story for some time,' he said, with something of his old, relaxed manner.

'That's a shame.' The words were meaningless, without conviction.

Once more he gazed over her shoulder, to the corner of the room where the boy had been. He was no longer there.

When they arrived at the television studios, Dane was ushered into the hospitality suite to meet the director of 'The Halloween Special', Gavin Connors. He also was young. Well, thought

Dane, to a man in his eighties, everyone's young. Gavin, as he insisted on being called, was dressed in cords and a large patterned sweater, and had a rather affected habit of constantly removing his unruly mop of hair from his eyes with a grand sweeping gesture. He spoke like Shara, with empty politeness.

'Great you could make it. It's a pleasure to be working with you,' he said in a well-practised fashion.

'Thank you,' said Dane.

'Now, Shara'll get you a drink – won't you sweetie? – and then about an hour from transmission, she'll bring you down to the studio. The plan is that Robert Glaiser will interview you about your writing – I'll introduce you later – and then we're going to see our version of "The Withered Rose". OK?'

Another quick shake of the hand and he was gone.

Dane began to wish he'd prepared himself more for this ordeal. Heavens, he couldn't even remember what 'The Withered Rose' was about.

'Now what can I get you, Mr Dane? Red wine, white wine, a G and T maybe?' Shara's white teeth flashed through her red lips.

'I'd love a cup of tea, if that would be possible,' he said.

Some time later a tall, dark-haired man came into the room and grabbed Dane's hand in a hearty shake. 'Bob Glaiser,' he announced, and paused as though waiting for applause. 'I'll be chatting to you on camera later on. I think it's always best if I have a few words with my victims beforehand.' He laughed a rehearsed laugh.

Dane nodded. 'I see. What is it you want me to say?'

'A little about your background. Talk about some of your best stories – except "The Withered Rose" of course. We want that to come as a complete surprise to the viewers.'

Dane felt a flood of relief.

'Don't worry,' continued Glaiser in his measured tones. 'Everything'll be fine. Just relax and enjoy yourself, It's only a bit of Halloween fun.' He made a sound like children make when they're imitating a ghost and then left.

Dane was glad to get some time to himself. He now rather regretted becoming involved in this television thing. He was too old for it all. The oldest ghost-story writer. His eyes misted for a moment.

The little boy on the platform turned and looked his way. He was dressed in a dull, grey gabardine with the belt tightly fastened and he clutched a shabby lunchbox in his hands. His velvet eyes looked appealingly at him. There was something terribly sad, terribly mournful and somehow familiar about him.

'Mr Dane. Time to go down to the studio. About thirty minutes from transmission.'

'Oh, right.'

'Having forty winks were we?' Gavin gave a fleeting, patronising smile and helped the writer to his feet. 'I expect it's a combination of the heat and the alcohol.'

'I haven't been drinking. I don't drink.'

Dane was taken to the control booth from where he could see two major sets: the mock interior of an old church and a book-lined study. 'That's where Bob will interview you, as though it's your own home.'

Dane was about to say that his home was not as grand as that, but decided not to bother. On the church set some technicians and actors were wandering about. A man dressed as a curate, obviously the star, was pacing up and down the aisle, apparently trying to remember his lines. A young woman dressed in a raincoat and headscarf was having some make-up powder applied to her nose. The set itself was impressive: it really looked like an old church, even down to the gnarled pews, altar candles and faded hangings.

His heart constricted and he grabbed the sides of his chair in order to control the sense of shock that overwhelmed him. For a moment, all sound ebbed away from him and he was left in a silent dreamworld. As he gazed at the five candles burning at the altar, he glimpsed a face gazing up at him through their ivory waxed fingers. It was the face of the little boy. There was no mistaking that face: the pale, doll-like features and those wide, staring eyes.

He blinked furiously to rid himself of this vision and looking again he saw just a vague shape moving at the rear of the set. The sound of the others in the control booth flooded back into his senses and, as he looked around, he saw that they had been too busy to notice his odd behaviour. He didn't want them to think he was going senile. He hoped he wasn't going senile. Perhaps he was, for he now knew who the child was – had – been. It was his brother Matthew. His little brother, who had died of diptheria at the age of nine. Or at least it was someone who looked like him. You really are getting your imagination back, he told himself wryly.

'OK, Mr Dane, we'll go down on the set and get you fixed up with a mike.'

'Tell me: is there a part for a schoolboy in this adaptation?'

'Schoolboy?' Gavin wrinkled his nose. 'No, only the curate, the mother and the policeman – just as in your story.'

The programme went better than Dane had expected. The interviewer knew his craft and drew a selection of interesting anecdotes out of him – most of which he thought he'd forgotten – and the adaptation of his story was rather good. Once it had started, he remembered the plot: how a withered rose blooms again as a signal to a young widow that her dead husband is in a happy place beyond death. Not one of his best stories, but the actors made a fine job of it. He was well pleased with the evening.

As he was about to leave the studios, Shara came rushing up to him, clutching an old, tatty paperback edition of *Grave Tales for Dark Nights*. 'This is my copy from my schooldays. Would you be so kind as to sign it, Mr Dane?'

Dane suddenly felt small and ungracious. He hadn't really cared for the girl, but obviously all that stuff she'd told him about admiring him and liking his work was true. Taking the copy, he inscribed the inside cover: 'To Shara, who looked after me one Halloween, best wishes, Montague Dane.'

The girl gave a contented squeal of delight and kissed him on the cheek. 'Goodbye. I do hope you start writing again soon.'

On his way home, he looked out of the railway carriage window into the moonless night. He saw little except for the far sprinkling of house lights in the distance, the shifting darker line of the horizon, and his own reflection staring back him from the blackness. It is a very old face now, he thought and sighed. I am a relic. That's how I've been treated today. Some old curiosity from a bygone age who's been wheeled out for his novelty value: the oldest living ghost-story writer in the land. The face in the railway carriage window creased into a sad smile. Life had gone on for too long.

His station was nearly deserted when he alighted from the train. He waited a few minutes while the other passengers trooped through the ticket barrier and the train had departed. He stood there in the chill wind, peering down the length of the empty platform, staring into the gloom. At regular intervals lamps threw down pale yellow puddles of light, but the rest was painted by the navy blue of the winter night.

Halloween: the time for ghosts.

Did something move at the far end of the platform? Was there a schoolboy there, in a tightly belted raincoat, clasping a lunchbox? Was it his brother?

Something was moving – towards him.

The wind stiffened and he shivered involuntarily. A figure, indefinable as yet, began to form at the far end of the platform. A vague silhouette shimmered in the gloom.

Dane clenched his fists and breathed deeply. 'Matthew,' he said faintly. 'Matthew.'

The figure emerged into one of the areas of light.

'Are you all right, sir?"

It was a porter.

'Yes. Yes, I'm all right. I just thought you were someone else.'

'Oh, welcome home to the television star,' cried Mrs Walters, Dane's housekeeper, when he came through the door.

'Did you watch it?'

'Course I did. You were very good. And that story of yours … well it had me sniffling at the end.'

Dane smiled, despite the strange feeling which was clouding his spirit.

'Now then,' chirruped Mrs Walters, 'what can I get you for supper?'

'Oh, nothing, thank you. The whole day has tired me out. I'm going straight to bed.'

But he did not sleep. He lay, propped up in bed, in the darkness, thinking. Thinking about his brother. He remembered the very last time he'd seen him. It was at the railway station. Matthew had stood in his blue raincoat, clutching his lunch box, reluctant to board the train. 'I don't want to go,' he'd said in that tiny, piping voice of his, the large blue eyes wet with tears. He was being sent to stay with Auntie Doris at the seaside. The fresh air was going to do him good.

But he never came back.

Dane had not thought about Matthew for years. The memories of him had faded like an old snapshot, and now here he was standing at the end of the bed, the pale moonlight falling softly on that fragile little face of his, the eyes glittering in their hollow sockets.

'Matthew,' Dane said in a whisper, no longer frightened, no longer haunted.

The little boy placed the lunch box on the bed and held out his arms to his brother.

Mrs Walters was surprised to find a scruffy old lunch box on the floor by Montague Dane's bed when she came to wake him the following morning. But she could not wake him. The oldest ghost-story writer in the land was dead.

18

THE RETURN

I returned – as I knew I would. There was an indissoluble link between me and Darkwood so that it was inevitable that I would visit the old place again. I just had to. After all it was where the most pivotal event in my life occurred.

And this was my anniversary.

I was drawn back on that misty May evening and stood in the fading light beneath the row of beech trees that skirted the lawn and gazed at the coloured lanterns strung around the patio area and the lights blazing from all the downstairs windows. I caught sounds of a jazz band floating out of the house on the gentle breeze. Some of the guests were dancing outside, filled with merriment and champagne.

The party was in full swing.

Gerald held the party at Darkwood to celebrate his birthday every year. It was always an extravagant affair. I had fond memories of the times I had been present in the past: the noise, the laughter, the sheer exuberance of it all. For a brief moment I was overcome by a wave of nostalgia, but I gently pushed these memories aside. They were worthless now.

I left the shadow of the trees and wandered across the lawn on to the patio. The giddy dancing guests took no notice of me. I slipped through the French windows and into the large hall where a quartet of musicians was playing. The area was full of people. Some were dancing, but most were just standing around in groups, drinks in hand, chatting merrily. Jokes were being made, secrets shared and gossip gathered.

Then I saw Gerald. He was leaning against a pillar, his arms around a pretty young girl. His face was pale and damp with sweat and his smile, as usual in these circumstances, was not quite convincing. However, it didn't surprise me that this slip of a thing seemed completely enraptured by him. The old Gerald Hamilton charm. I knew all about that. Smooth, hypnotic, enticing and cold as ice. No doubt he was telling her that she was the love of his life.

I watched them for a while. Watched until he leered forward and kissed the girl on the lips. She responded with enthusiasm.

The fool, I thought.

I moved around the edge of the room towards the staircase, hoping that Gerald would not see me. But there was little danger of that happening. His attention was focused solely on the girl. I knew that obsessive mind of his. I had been the object of it once upon a time.

I slipped upstairs unseen and made my way to Gerald's bedroom, his passion suite as he used to refer to it. The term amused me then. But not now. The room was very much as I remembered it. The décor had not changed, not even the carpet. Well, it was only a year. The sheets were rumpled and an empty bottle of champagne rested in a silver bucket by the side of the bed. Lovemaking had taken place here earlier this evening. The flighty piece downstairs, no doubt, the one who hung on his every word and gesture. The old Gerald magic. He'd send her off on a cloud of romance into the night and she'd never realise how she had been used.

I sat in a chair opposite the bed for quite some time, somewhat mesmerised by the unnaturally faded patch on the carpet near the bed. Eventually, I opened the French windows and stepped out on to the balcony, which overlooked the gravel drive. Some of the guests were leaving. Expensive motors revved their engines and headlights pierced the dark as, like will o' the wisps, they made their erratic way down the winding tree-lined drive.

Another hour, I thought, and he'll be left in the house alone. Alone that is apart from me.

It was around two in the morning when Darkwood fell silent. All guests, musicians, flunkeys and lovers had gone. I had Gerald to myself at last. I waited in the deep shadows by the curtain. I could hear his uncertain footsteps approaching the bedroom. Gerald never got really drunk, but he was often tipsy. He entered. He was rather dishevelled: his bow tie was crooked, one flap of his shirt hung down over the front of his trousers and his hair was in disarray. He was humming to himself. It was a happy little tune. He sat on the bed to take his shoes off.

I moved forward into the pool of light created by the moonbeams spilling into the room. So concentrated was he in removing his recalcitrant shoes that he didn't notice me.

'Hello, Gerald,' I said softly, moving to the left of him.

He looked up, surprised to hear a voice in the room and swivelled his head anxiously to discover its owner. Then he saw me. His eyes bulged and his jaw dropped.

'Aren't you going to say hello?' I purred.

He rose to his feet like a man who has just learned to walk and staggered backwards in some distress towards the French windows.

'It is our anniversary, after all, Gerald,' I said. 'It's been a year.'

His mouth opened and closed, his teeth champing noisily, but he spoke no words.

'Yes, a whole year,' I continued. 'A whole year since you shot me. Murdered me in cold blood. And talking of blood, I see that you managed to clean up the stain quite well. There's not a trace of red there now.' I pointed at the faded patch on the carpet.

Gerald clamped his hands to side of his face and shook his head. 'I must be dreaming,' he gabbled, as he stumbled backwards on to the balcony.

I approached him, smiling. 'No dream, Gerald. This is all happening. Happy anniversary.'

'Keep … keep away,' he moaned, his back now against the parapet.

'That's no way to talk to the woman you called the love of your life, is it Gerald? I am the love of your life, aren't I?'

It amused me to see that he had no idea how to answer that question.

'Give me a kiss for old times' sake?' I murmured, moving very close to him. I was close enough to smell the fear. I caressed his face with my hand.

He gave a scream of terror, leaning away from me until he lost his balance. With a pleasing inevitability he slipped over the edge of the parapet. His arms and legs flailing, he fell to the drive below and his head smashed like an eggshell on contact with the hard surface. Blood oozed out on to the gravel. I looked down and wondered how difficult it would be to remove that stain.

ABOUT THE
AUTHOR

DAVID STUART DAVIES left teaching to become editor of
Sherlock magazine and is generally regarded as an expert on
Sherlock Holmes, having written seven novels, film books
and plays featuring the character. He has given presentations
on Holmes at many festivals and conferences as well as on
board *Queen Mary II*. He also created two detectives: wartime
private eye Johnny Hawke, who has appeared in six novels,
and Huddersfield-based Detective Inspector Paul Snow, in a
series of dark thrillers, the first two of which are *Brothers in Blood*
and *Innocent Blood*. David is a member of the Crime Writers
Association, editing their monthly magazine *Red Herrings*. He is
also currently general editor for Wordsworth's *Tales of Mystery
& the Supernatural* series and has written many introductions to
classic ghost-story collections, including those by the master of
the genre, M.R. James. For the past ten years, David has met with
a group of writing friends in York during the festive season to
read their own spooky tales. A number of the stories featured in
this volume had their first airing at these meetings. David lives in
Huddersfield, West Yorkshire with his wife Kathryn.
www.davidstuartdavies.co.uk

Also from The History Press

We are proud to present our history crime fiction imprint, The Mystery Press, featuring a dynamic and growing list of titles written by diverse and respected authors, united by the distinctiveness and excellence of their writing. From a collection of thrilling tales by the CWA Short Story Dagger award-winning Murder Squad, to a Victorian lady detective determined to solve some sinister cases of murder in London, these books will appeal to serious crime fiction enthusiasts as well as those who simply fancy a rousing read.

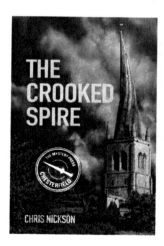

Find these titles and more at
www.thehistorypress.co.uk

Also from The History Press

HAUNTED

This series is sure to petrify everyone interested in the ghostly history of their hometown. Containing a terrifying collection of spine-chilling tales, from spooky sightings in pubs and theatres to paranormal investigations in cinemas and private homes, each book in the series is guaranteed to appeal to both serious ghost hunters and those who simply fancy a fright.

Also from The History Press

More Spooky Books